Also by Marc Estrin

<u>Novels</u>
Speckled Vanities
And Kings Shall Be Thy Nursing Fathers
The Prison Diaries of Alan Kreiger (Terrorist)
When The God Come Home To Roost
Tsim-Tsum
The Good Doctor Guillotin
Skulk
The Annotated Nose
Golem Song
The Lamentations of Julius Marantz
The Education of Arnold Hitler
Insect Dreams: The Half Life of Gregor Samsa

<u>Memoir</u>
Rehearsing With Gods: Photographs and Essays
on the Bread and Puppet Theater
(with Ron Simon, Photographer)

Hyde

Marc Estrin

Fomite
Burlington, VT

Image credits:
Cover image: Ceres Occator Crater & Carbonates, NASA
Page 207: © Sedmak Dreamstime.com - Lithography Of Christ Resurrection Photo (Lithography of Christ resurrection by Albert Durer)
All other images by the author

ISBN-13: 978-1-942515-35-7
Library of Congress Control Number: 2016944431
Fomite
58 Peru Street
Burlington, VT 05401
www.fomitepress.com

Philosophy is odious and obscure;
Both law and physic are for petty wits;
Divinity is basest of the three,
Unpleasant, harsh, contemptible, and vile.
'Tis magic, magic that hath ravished me.

Marlowe, Doctor Faustus

"Everybody's got a plan until they get punched in the mouth."

Mike Tyson

ME, LITTLE MR. HYDE

I was never a truly nice person. But then again I never wanted to be one. Now, of course, I am beyond good or evil. *Mysterium tremendum.*

Et exempli gratia: I always thought feces were a really get-ahead idea, a way to achieve all and whatever. Even as an infant, bald as an egg, I preferred poop to slobber. Loading my diapers was great fun. Watching my parents change them was the best part.

Maybe it was my dad who gave me the idea. 'Shit!', I remember him saying when he first saw the blue blanket in my incubator. He'd wanted a daughter. I know this, because he often told me so later. But burned into my mind's eye is his saying 'Shit!' while staring at me. Granted, it could have been a command rather than a descriptor. What did I know at that age? I couldn't hear him through the glass, but I remember clearly his lip movements — the pursing of the lips to make the shh sound, and the precipitate closing of them for the plosive T. What other word could it have been? At that formative time in my education, it stuck with me.

I thought about it often as I played with my infant and toddler poops, being able to shape them before I could shape much else. They were the 1921 version of Playdoh, ten years *avant la lettre*. They would stick to walls. I could throw them at my parents and evoke disgusted amusement far more quickly than simply wailing my lungs out like some crazed banshee.

So, being a smart little thing, I quickly learned that the way to get my way was by throwing shit at people, which I later understood as a metaphor with broader application, and in colors more variegated than yellow or brown.

At the tender age when I was still saying Pa-pa and Ma-ma and sticking my fingers into fire, at that very age, I thought myself to have observed everything and to have already seen deep into men's hearts. Ever needy, inclined to violent tantrums, but still without the complexities of speech, I sucked greedily on all the melancholies of the world to force my maturation. It, however, from the confines of my crib, was not as forthcoming as the nipple. "Hey you, I'm thirsty. How about a drink?" And she always complied.

See? One begins with small demands, taking advantage of female kindness. But the further prospects are huge, if one draws the right lessons, which it turns out I did. Three cheers for Cause and Effect.

As an important man — I knew I was to be one, even in my baby dreams — I was always drawn to creative behavior. Destructive-creative, perhaps, but how else to conjure progress? For instance, I was bombarded with nursery rhymes, most of which were adequately realistic, like Humpty Dumpty or Jack and Jill, but one of which sticks in my mind as a particularly creative prompt. I'm sure you know this one:

The grand old Duke of York,

He had ten thousand men.

Yes, that may be true (it may not be. I was still innocent of historical research) — but then, what did he do with them?

He marched them up to the top of the hill,

And he marched them down again.

This rhyme pointed me early on to a key perception of The Human Problem. Corollary? Everything, no matter what, had to be reevaluated.

The poem continues, and reveals its skill at unconscious self-parody.

And when they were up, they were up,

And when they were down, they were down,

(Both empty tautologies. But here is the clincher:)

And when they were only half-way up,

They were neither up nor down.

Has there ever been a more incisive depiction of human inadequacy, of the root cause of everything wrong with the world?

Of course I changed the text as soon as I could articulate the syllables, and — in my three-year old manner — understand its implications.

The grand old Duke of York,

He had a lot of men.

He marched them up to the top of the hill,

And he ate them in his den.

There. Don't you think this is more realistic, not to mention more reflective, on the part of a small child?

The success of this exercise led directly to some of my early pubescent works for which the high-school-Hyde was dubbed an "intellectual", yclept Most Likely to Make Big Bucks, though the relationship between the two is usually inversely proportional. I have to say that my edition of *Crime and Punishment Without the Punishment,* which I created by simply tearing the paperback off at page 93 and discarding the rest, sold quite well at Rutgers, and paid more than twice the outlay for the uncorrected edition — probably because the students felt they could get away with reading only 17% of the book, and thereby be able to fake their way through classes and short essay questions.

But I am getting ahead of myself.

Once out of infancy, I had to revolt into something, so I revolted into something age-appropriate — sanity. I devoted myself thoroughly to the multiplication tables, and devoured whatever printed thing I met with — cereal boxes, small print on patent medicines, legal notices on the bottom of mattresses. I was pronounced a "genius" by the principal of my elementary school. For punishment, he had my IQ measured in a grueling series of tests, and labeled me "163", his name for me henceforth — and my prisoner number, pinioned in the bastille of high expectations. His appended note to my report card: "Charles demonstrates an inward vivacity that promises much." Vivacious, yes, of course, but I remained a long while merely a feral infant prodigy, tormented by some indefinable hunger.

I imagined the answer lay in crime. But my career as a petty thief ended abruptly when Maud, my mother, made me go back to Harry's, apologize personally face to face to Harry, and return the pack of Juicy Fruit I had filched. I was stupidly considerate enough to offer her a stick. Of course she interrogated me like a pro from Pyongyang, and turned me in. My own mother. This was a lesson about mothers and women in general. Never again.

But as embarrassment faded, I still thought I might take part in some universal Harmony of the Crooked.

Why?

Again, a childhood implant:

There was a crookèd man, and he walked a crookèd mile,

He found a crookèd sixpence against a crookèd stile;

He bought a crookèd cat which caught a crookèd mouse,

And they all lived together in a little crookèd house.

Is that a marvelously harmoniously image, or what? What's not to relish?

I could, I *would* be a crookèd man when I grew up. In fact, the crookèd man drawn in my book was far more interesting looking than Liam, my father, or Nelson L. Goodwin, the principal who so admired my genius. And, admit it: all miles are crookèd, are they not, and all money, according to my father, so that was no big deal. A crookèd cat and crookèd mouse? — that might be interesting for a crookèd cat & mouse game. But. But, but, but. — I didn't want a crookèd house. No, sireee. That shack in the picture looked to be on its last legs.

I don't mean to put my father down. I loved him — in a sort of sine curvy way, but I came to realize that his being "strong-willed" — as my mother would say — didn't quite elevate him to the level of passable. Most of what he accomplished in his too-short life didn't, in my opinion, rise beyond the level of simple shrewdness. I knew I would surpass him.

But I didn't get a chance to really muscle up to him, since God spoke, and both he and my mother moved on during the flu epidemic of '29, an event that made a big impression on me. I was nine, Aunt Betsy's new possession, by which time I had a jackknife, my version of a sword — the most basic tool of childhood. But there were other things I needed that cost money — a baseball glove, a bat and ball, a football, a basketball, model cars and planes, a bike, a BB-gun and fireworks. So, since Betsy's 10¢/week allowance would hardly suffice, I would need a continuing outside source of money.

Most of my other needs were out there in the wilds of

Paterson, New Jersey — nails, acorns, bottle tops, crab apples, rocks, dirt, grass, snow, firewood and cans. Other more extraordinary supplies were available because we lived near a mill on the Passaic that made woolen goods and cheap jewelry. All manners of wood, glass and wire abounded. As boys, we had to be able to start a fire, make a good snowball (sometimes implanted with a rock), climb trees, lie, hide, swear, spit, throw a knife and fight. Basic sports skills were also required, the more spectacular, the better.

You know what was great? From the mill we heisted industrial-sized spools of thread to weave webs across side streets with not much traffic, hoping to catch cars. But of course the cars broke right through the thread. My friend Andy was more adventurous. He strung his web across Main Street and was killed by a '26 Desoto. That wasn't so great. I heard the crash but I didn't see him get hit. He was the only person I knew who was dead. Beside my parents.

After my short career as car-trapper and petty thief, my still-alive mother decided I'd better join the Cub Scouts so as to get me back on the straight and narrow. Shortsighted again. My first merit badge did me in. I had to walk 12 feet on the edge of a two by four. I practiced on a railing at the entrance to the park by the Falls. I spent hours practicing but was never able to walk the whole 12 feet. Maybe I was developmentally deficient, without a cerebellum or something. Other kids seemed to be able to do it. So my father, a neurotically honest goody-two-shoes like my mother, wouldn't sign my damn merit badge form. Too dishonest for him, don'tcha know. I suspected all the other parents of merit badgers were more lenient, but I didn't know for sure. I never went it any farther in cub scouts. I sold my uniform and cub scout manual for more than we had paid for it. But I did become the most hypocritical altar boy in the history of St. Michael's Royal Crown Church

What else? What else? Imagination, help me overcome the contrivance of these memoirs. I have not said everything yet; I am coming up to things more important.

1. RELIGION

My early religious experience was quite profound. I didn't know enough to be underwhelmed by the incense, the great St. Mike's organ, and the Latin gobbledygook intoned by Father Mulvaney.

And the choir. St. Mike's was no hymn-singing musical backwoods. I didn't know it then since I had known no other church, but the choir was led by the now-famous Dr. Theodor Grudzinski, at the time a grad student in musicology at Rutgers, who brought along his sight-singing girlfriends and ringers to goose up our local wailers. Tallis and Palestrina, Josquin, Obrecht, and Schutz, Monteverdi and Lassus and whoever the hell else. But no 19th-century musical bums, let me tell you. And with Grudzinski at the organ, only Bach — J.S., and not any of his piddling children.

In my dark childhood years, that music was a source of light which put all my hunger in its place way better than the hot dogs at Libby's, over at the Falls. Of which I still eat four or five a week.

It was as if my mind had electrical feelers for those sound

waves. And the feelers connected not just to my ears, but into my eyes and up the optic nerves to my reptilian brain. Medulla rapture. Throbbing pulse. Ever more yearning. Really religious stuff.

I didn't understand "soul" at that point, but something in me felt like it was being filled with helium. I would have floated off the pew if I hadn't been worried about embarrassing my parents in front of their friends. But I imagined those feeling as the "pious thoughts", the "holy bliss" Father Mulvaney preached and the grownups talked about.

The "Fall" too. That worried me. The Fall of Man. Growing up near the Great Passaic Falls, I had a well-developed sense of the vertical. I'd often experienced the heart-stopping fear of hurtling down those 55 feet into the thunderous crashing of the water on the rocks below. I clung to the guard rail, but still felt the overwhelming water dragging at me to follow.

Like the cloud of spray filling the void at the bottom, my understanding of the Fall was unclear. It had something to do with apples — which I liked, especially the yellow ones — and with naked — which I was every time I sat in the washtub and Mama poured hot water over me — so I realized that falling the Fall was not just for other people, but had something to do with me. Especially when I failed my balance beam merit badge. And I thought it would be better to not. Fall. But there, there was no obvious railing to hold onto. Only one to walk on.

The worst was when I got older, nine or ten, and I was

even an altar boy. Some altar boy! I found myself listening to the celestial music, and imagining the most beautiful Rutgers girls naked under their blue robes. Is there such a thing as unparalleled sinfulness? By then I understood "soul", and I was rewarded with this? Understanding the horror of my soul in the sight of God?

One beauty was singing about the Virgin Mary, and I was imagining her breasts, her naked breasts, rising and falling with her breathing. And when she would hold her music up so I couldn't see them, her breasts, I would curse her, no matter how beautifully she was intoning *"O Mater Dei, memento mei"*.

I could die for thinking this, I thought at the end of the piece. God might strike me dead, and I mumbled ten Hail Marys in a row to ward Him off. And when it was time, I ran out of the church, stumbling on the steps as my sinful thoughts chased me with flaming sword.

O Mater Dei, gimme a break! I didn't mean it, those thoughts. I don't know why I thought them. I swear to God I'll never think such thoughts again.

Fat chance. I was a sinner. An altar boy sinner — the worst kind. Surely I was condemned to Hell.

We altar boys used to sing

The Bells of Hell go ding-a-ling-a-ling for you, and not for me.

O Death where is thy sting-a-ling-a-ling, O grave, thy victory?

Not any more. The way to hell was paved with mortal sins. If thinking of Annabelle's tits wasn't a mortal sin, what was?

Hell is not a thought one can live with, especially a genius kid like me. Read *Portrait of the Artist* if you want to understand what we Irish kids were fed. I won't go into it here, it's too hair-raising. 70 million trillion years of burning? Even one year would be a long time. But my revolt into sanity protected me. My sword and shield. *Ein feste Burg ist unser Gott*, we sang. And God had his ways of protecting me.

Distinguo.

Not every sin is a mortal sin. Some are mere venial sins, though the word "venial" sounds much worse than mortal. I began a serious consideration of which of the many sins I had committed were mortal. Any single one, like the Annabelle's-tits-sin for instance, might be excused in that wonderful device standing in a corner, that carved, dark box of the Confessional. But a whole life pattern? The vast majority being mortal? Not even the Pope could pardon such a thing. What, after all, would Hell be for if not for that kind of a life?

To make up for Annabelle's delicious tits, I decided to write my own *Summa Theologica*, the first section being an examination of my behavior with respect to the Ten Commandments, which, as my Catechism noted, are "those conditions of a life freed from the slavery of sin." The slavery of sin — not for me. How was I doing so far?

1. I am the LORD your God. Worship the Lord your God and Him only shall you serve. Hmm. I kind of worshipped Babe Ruth. I had pictures of him all over my room, and baseball cards. But I didn't really serve him the way I served at mass. So I guessed I was ok.

2. Thou shalt not take the name of the Lord your God in vain. Well, damn! I must have said Goddamn it four to ten times a day, depending on how things were going. And Jesus Christ! But was that mortal or venial? Venial, I guessed. So again I was all right.

3. Remember to keep holy the Sabbath day. I don't think baseball is *un*holy. And I was sure God didn't think so either, or He wouldn't have allowed it to be invented.

4. Honor your father and your mother. I was ok there, I think, until they died, and after that, I didn't feel Aunt Betsy counted as much, not to get all legalistic about it. But four down. So far so good.

5. Thou shalt not kill. OK, don't kill people, maybe, I got that, and I'd never killed anyone anyway. But what about shooting a hurt horse which my friend Horace's father did, or putting down an old dog, or shooting squirrels which everyone does, and if you take that further, accidentally stepping on bugs or worms while you're walking, or washing the germs off your hands down the sink? Humans may be different, made in God's image, but as for the rest, it was a *reductio ad absurdum*, proving my killing sins were venial, not mortal.

6. Thou shalt not commit adultery. What did I know about adultery? I thought the word meant something like trying to get into a bar when you were only a kid. Six down.

7. Thou shalt not steal. Bingo on that. But maybe God has something like "petty larceny" and "grand larceny". If so, only "grand" would be mortal, right? And "petty" would

chalk up as venial. So I was out by the skin of my teeth —
assuming God made such distinctions, which I'm sure He did.

8. Thou shalt not bear false witness against your neighbor.
What did that mean? Being called up to the stand in some
trial and telling a lie? I was too young to be called. And just
how picky were they? If the kid I was lying about lived a
couple of blocks away? I was pretty sure I was all right with
that one. Almost there. Pretty good so far.

9. Thou shalt not covet your neighbor's wife. I wasn't
sure what "covet" exactly was, but whatever it was — Mrs.
Wright? Mrs. Faletti? No way. They were both fat and ugly
and besides they were too old for me.

10. I can't remember what 10 was, but if it's tenth on a list
of ten, it couldn't be all that important.

So:

A+, Charlie Hyde. Or at least A. Or maybe B+. But my
life — again excluding Annabelle's tits — was not all that
blameworthy. Hell was not in my future.

But what about Purgatory? The Catechism told the
requirements for heaven: a soul had to be absolutely clean,
with no blemish of sin. OK. I could work on that before I
died with the help of the Booth. But what if I was not quite
clean enough for heaven, but not foul enough for Hell — like
with my propensity for venial sins, I was likely to be, especially if I was hit by a truck before I could get to confession?
Seemed to me that was a likely ticket to Purgatory.

Graduating from purgatory might mean acceptance in

heaven, maybe, but purgatory also had its burning apparatus, except not forever ones. Just until the sins were burned away enough to make it into heaven. That could be a long time, depending on how long it was between confessing and all the venial sins that might have slipped in since. And even one second of burning couldn't be too nice.

So I figured I had to do something about the Purgatory thing. The way to shorten purgatory according to the catechism was by good works, prayer, fasting and abstinence. In general, good works were probably out, at least the ones Father Mulvaney was always harping on. I didn't usually know anyone who was sick, and if I did, my mother probably wouldn't let me visit them because I might catch it. I had never clothed the naked because I had never even seen any naked people except myself and imagining Annabelle, and I always got dressed again as quickly as possible. She probably did, too. There was the men's locker room at the swimming pool, but people always stood facing the wall, and a bare ass is not much in my opinion, and besides, I couldn't really just grab their clothes and hand them to them. I never buried the dead because undertakers did that. And I never gave alms to the poor because I had only my 10¢ a week for myself. You see what I mean? A kid in Paterson in the twenties didn't have much chance to do good deeds. I once got my father a key chain for his birthday with a rabbit's foot on it, but that got canceled out because he said it was superstitious and against the First Commandment. You just couldn't win.

But if you couldn't win, you could take your ball and go home. Home was sanity, right? If the First Commandment said you had to worship God, why were people worshiping statues? If I blinked twice it looked like idolatry to me. I tried to question several old ladies about what they were doing on their knees. They thought I was cute. But I wasn't cute. I was an eleven-year old Kierkegaard. As in my infancy, I looked around with non-benevolent curiosity, collecting evidence against the world, at first the world of St. Michael the Archangel, and later, of course, against the world at large.

As with the Buddha, its misery became ever more apparent. Sickness, old age, pain and death. My ineluctable conclusion was that the world could not be the work of an all-loving beneficent God. It must have been a co-production with the devil, or at least some deity who loved suffering. Or why else would people so persistently give up the churchy path? What did they know that I and the kneeling ladies, didn't?

This was so disturbing a question that I prayed a lot for the answer. Down on my knees, even. O Lord Jesus Christ, and his mother, and Joseph, also, please have mercy on me, a poor sinner, a smarter-than-normal, but regular human being, and slip me the answer to the Big Question: how come the world is so shitty?

I didn't phrase it like that, even though, as you can imagine "shitty" was hardly a derogatory term in my book. I don't remember exactly how I put it, but the answer hovered vaguely above my head and in my nostrils, and I didn't like the way it smelled. I thought I'd give a first try to good works as a way to change the world and shorten my time in purgatory. I signed up for a course at the YMCA to become a lifeguard. I passed, as usual, with flying colors.

The trouble with actually being a life guard is that you see humanity in its worst incarnations — except for some of the girls. I worked for four mid-teen summers at the Sunnyside Pool over on Grand St. It was a three story building with a huge whitewashed wall surrounding the pool. You could see the top of the high board and huge slide from across the street. It took up a whole square block, and was always packed since it was right on the trolley line. Also because there were so many people out of work, what else was there to do for 10¢? You got changed in one of the locker rooms, and went out into the pool area. I never did find out what was on the upper floors, but now that I think about it, those floors were probably up to no good.

The shallow end was generally utilized by parents ambitious to turn their babies into Johnny Weismullers or Esther Williamses so they could support them in their old age. Perhaps they expected their kids to grow gills or webs between their toes to better compete in the Olympics. The little ones, unlike their parents, had an amusing miniature air of dignity, since they hadn't lived long enough to become grotesque. Other shallow enders were hideous overweight eldsters who would waddle down the steps into the water, and a variegated zoo of non-normals who would stand and screech, or do endless laughing jumping jacks, or just turn and turn in place Because the water began at three feet, and went only to four feet before it was roped off, these inhabitants did not bear all that much watching. The non-normals, or feebs, as we lifeguards called them, usually had their feeb-keepers as first responders.

Well and good, that left time and space to concentrate on the mid-range of the pool, the hangout of the lovely young girls and the leering beau brummels that lounged around their flesh like sharks. I, of course, was one of them, but I was up on my high chair, a heroic dive away, and behind sunglasses under a pith helmet. (I don't know why it was called that, unless it was a lisping corruption of piss, as in pissing on the natives.) (I am very interested in etymology.)

Those girls were not in choir gowns, let me tell you. The twenties had not happened in vain. So much enticing skin out there for frolicking and tanning. Legs to mid-thigh, bare arms and lovely shoulders. And breasts galore beckoning from under form-fitting fabric. Even an occasional midriff gleaming up at me. I could blow my whistle all I wanted, and gesture with my arms, but it's a good thing I never had to make a rescue, to stand up and draw attention to that thing poking the front of my swim trunks. The red cross badge sewn onto the leg might distract an elderly eye, but I was sure the lovelies would zoom right onto the main event. Blowing my whistle and hiding my woodie for four long summers didn't exactly qualify as good works.

But something good did come out of my sun-drenched summers at Sunnyside: I was watching the disgusting shark-boys, my rivals, show off to the fleshlings below by jumping, and occasionally diving from the high board. I was keeping my eye on one particularly hateful swain, a narcissistically slick dago with seriously developed muscles, and a tight, red, one-piece suit — probably his younger brother's — which emphasized his bulge, far more attractive than mine. I studied all of him carefully though my binoculars. Very close-set eyes. I'm no expert physiognomist, but even then I knew enough to suspect that his face was affected by a small collapse of his skull where the faculties of conscience were normally located.

He would walk out to the end of the board, survey the eyes looking up at him, then, in case some lovely had missed his understated approach, he would "test" the board, by jumping several times, each time higher, never slipping, never ripping his groin to shreds as one leg slid off the board, finally absorbing the rebound with his knees, and turning back to begin a full approach. By this time, there was not a single pair of female eyes not glued to his body, and probably focused on the bulge below his waist. I gritted my teeth, hoping he would do himself some serious damage. But up he went, and instead of swan-diving as was his wont, he curved backwards at the peak of his jump, and just missing the board with his nose (and his bulge) descended in perfect form, toes and fingers pointed, and I watched him plunge under the water.

Perhaps it was the sun in my eyes, perhaps an aesthetic thrill at such perfection, perhaps it was jealousy, perhaps extreme disappointment that the board hadn't sheared off the front half of his body, but somewhere in the course of that dive (here's the good part) I experienced a time coulisse, a slippage out of the present to a formative moment of awe from childhood. The door of ten years was flung open, and there I was at the Paramount Theater in Newark on October 11, 1926. I know that was the day because my father and mother took me to see The Great Houdini as a surprise for my sixth birthday. A big Saturday night out in the city. I took a nap so I'd be able to stay up late.

What I remember most, now, forty odd years later, is of course, the climax of the show, Houdini's famous and to this day unexplained Chinese Water Torture escape. This Newark show turned out to be late in the magician's career. In fact, it may have been his last show. A few days later, on Halloween, he was dead, a fact that changed my life for a while, and even today accounts for my admirable abdominals. My parents explained both China and torture to me on the drive in. Needless to say I found both extremely interesting.

The velour curtain of that fantastic, sculptured room, my first auditorium except the one at St. Michael's Archangel Elementary, went up to reveal a cabinet a little taller than I was, something like a small glass phonebooth, half-filled with water, standing on a waterproof sheet like the one I used when I wet the bed, but bigger. There was a huge ax nearby which made me think that maybe they would chop off his head and Houdini would put it back on.

The magician came onstage in a tuxedo. He was small, a tiny man, but I was used to that after seeing him do astounding tricks for the last hour. He said there was nothing supernatural about what he was about to do, and that he would offer $1,000 to anyone who could prove that it was possible to breathe inside the torture cell when he was in it and it filled with water. He explained that the ax was for his assistants who would break open the tank if it was necessary to save his life. They knew how long he could hold his breath. Exciting!

He showed how the top fit onto the water cell, and how it would be impossible to open from the inside even if were not locked. Grownups came up from the audience to inspect the torture cell, my father among them, so I knew it wasn't just his confederates.

His assistants climbed on two step-ladders, and filled the tank the rest of the way from buckets standing onstage, while Houdini went off to change into a blue bathing suit. Lots of muscles, like the Adonis on the high board. He lay down in front of the glass cell, and his ankles were locked into a stock from which he could not escape. My father swore his feet could not possibly wriggle out without unlocking. He was then placed in a small, tight cage, hooked to ropes from the flies. A winch in the wings slowly lifted the stock and cage off the mat, a dangerous move, which Houdini explained might break his ankles if done wrong. He was raised up until he hung directly over the water cell, head down, took some deep breaths and gave the signal to lower him, upside down, into the water with his arms folded across his chest, and his head touching its bottom. People in the front row got spilled on, as he over-filled the tank. A steel lid was squeezed down over the cell and padlocked, leaving his bare feet exposed above.

A curtain was drawn around the cell, an assistant stood by with the ax, and the orchestra played menacing music. After one minute, Houdini came around from the side of the cur-tain, drew it aside, and showed the torture cell still locked with the unspilled water still remaining. The audience, including me, went wild. When I quizzed my parents on the drive home, my mother thought that he must have used some kind of "dema-terialization" to pass through the glass, and then rematerialize onstage. I had not thought she might be kidding.

The only thing I could compare it to was Christ rising from the dead, but my parents got angry, and said it was just a trick, and that he wasn't really locked in. "But," I tried to argue with my father, "you said he was, that you saw it with your own eyes, and felt the wood and the steel and tried the locks with your own hands." "I lied," he said.

Either he was lying, or he was lying about lying, and both were a sin, the first probably venial, but the second possibly mortal, because of its double nature. That my parents were surely sinners was the first lesson of my birthday evening.

The second lesson gathered itself gradually around the earlier part of the show, a series of less spectacular, less death-defying, but nonetheless impressive magic. Swallowing needles and thread and bringing up threaded needles made me worry about Houdini's intestines — which turned out to be prophetic. But the combination of walking through a wall, and the subsequent water escape made me realize that if I could learn those tricks I could go anywhere, get anything, and if caught, get out of any handcuffs or lockups. While I was still small, it would just be something like locked cabinets at school, or closed candy stores, but when I got older, bigger, stronger, there was no limit to what wall penetration or escape arts might bring. In my childish way, this was my moment of *felix culpa*. There lurked in my heart the faintest sketch of a career. I was really happy to think about such possibilities. I wasn't born in the wake of the 1919 World Series fix for nothing.

2. THE YOUNG MR. HYDE

St. Mike's Archangel Elementary was not as elementary or as archangelic as it sounded. For one thing, in its Romish recalcitrance, it had refused to accept the new secular, developmental distinction between big boys and little boys. I imagine they thought us all equally deceiving scum in the eyes of God, so there would be no junior high school in our diocese. SMA Elementary contained boys grades 1-8.

That is, it *tried* to contain them. My early faith in the human race was born, fed, and developed by continuing creative insolence in the face of brutal control. If the Allied armies had consisted only of Catholic ex-youth, fascism would have been scotched in its cradle. Or in the case of SMA-E, Irished or Italianed, *vernichtet*, as Hitler used to say.

What also was not so elementary was the sophistication of toadying and bullying that went on among us. One point of particular pain for me was my name, a common Irish one. But the smart Italian kids would not let up. From the third grade on, over-Jesuitical, italianate eight- or nine-year olds, precociously literary, began pointing fingers at this little shrimp kid, and calling him "Mr. Hyde", or more commonly "Mr. Hy-yde" with that falling minor third universal in teasing songs. "Here comes Mister Hy-yde…Here comes Mister Hy-yde…" repeat *ad infinitum*, or until stopped by a well-meaning nun, usually sadistic in her own right. That is, if nuns were actually "her" — I wasn't sure. They had high voices, but…were they even human?

The reason for all this teasing was a complete mystery to me. Aunt Betsy Hyde was as mystified as I. But one Saturday when I was 12, the answer came flooding over me — for only 15¢ — from the silver screen at a Paterson Loews matinée. I knew I would find it there: the film was called *Dr. Jekyll and Mr. Hyde*. Mister Hyde, Mister Hy-yde, a film about somebody with my name! I begged a quarter from Auntie, and promised to explain what the fuss was all about.

I bought popcorn with my extra dime, put my pad and penlight on my lap (I was prepared to take notes) and settled in, my feet up on the seat in front of me until the matron came and told me to get my feet down. "What do you think this is, your home?" she hissed. The funny thing was that Aunt Betsy's house was the last place in the entire universe I would put my feet up.

The screen flickered, 8, 7, 6, 5, 4, 3, a two second gray space and then a mountain appeared, piercing the clouds, haloed by stars:

A Paramount Picture,

then

ADOLPH ZUKOR PRESENTS
Fredric March in
DR. JEKYLL AND MR. HYDE
A Rouben Mamoulian Production

I waited.

Bach! The G minor fugue. String transcription, but still…
beloved Bach! Get on with the titles, please, I don't know
these people. Robert Louis Stevenson…I've heard of him.
Ah, organ, hands on organ, that's the real Grudzinski sound.

It's hard to know how many of you today have seen this
masterpiece. When goddamn MGM decided to film another
Jekyll and Hyde with Spencer Tracy in '41, they bought the
Mamoulian rights from Paramount, withdrew all distribution
and stuck the negative in their vaults. No competition for
them, the capitalist pigs. But on that day in 1932 I saw the
entire haunting, penetrating, erotic work, and was penetrated
thenceforth.

My mind reeled. A plan to separate human good from
human evil! Yes. If you could only do that, you could somehow corral the evil and defang it while the better half stayed
free to build a brave new world. (I was still idealistic at twelve.)
And even though my name was Hyde, the doctor was just
like me: "It's the things one can't do that always tempt me."
I scribbled that down in the dark, since I knew the matron
would catch me using my penlight. Illegibly, it turned out,
but that's approximately what he said. He talked about the

girl, the blond girl, her leg, her leg dangling in his mind. Like Anabella's tits for me in church. I already knew something bad would ensue. "There are no bounds"? Ha!

I watched the exemplary scientist mix his beakers. I watched through flame and bubbling liquid, and noticed the skeleton in the corner of the lab. And then, the agony of transformation. Jekyll-March, the hitherto matinée idol, now a dark, fanged monster with wide-set eyes. What were his first words? "Free! Free at last!" "Free at last!" Words I would look to throughout my life.

Hyde — that's me! — looks at himself in the mirror, grins, laughs, stretches, dances, and gets gleefully dressed. Out into the rain, agile as a cat. Except in Paterson, not London. He takes off his top hat and lets the drops cover his face. He opens his mouth for a drink from heaven, just the way I do. Such happiness, such boundless joy in the created world! "Free at last!"

"You're an angel," the girl tells him, she of the dangling leg, he of the inner fang.

Doctor Jekyll sits in the park, listening to the birds, warily watching a black cat stalking. The cat springs, tears into the songbird's throat — and Jekyll's hands begin to darken at this hint of Nature's true essence. The rosy world, is it? Or fang, claw, and darkness?

The horrifying end, the caped fall from crucifixion. The mob gathers round, and stares amazed at the metamorphosis of monster to man, calm and beautiful — in death. Free at last.

I staggered from the theater. What had I learned? About me?

For one, I now realized what the kids were singing about: "Here comes Mister Hy-yde…Here comes Mister Hy-yde…" And I *was* Mr. Hyde, or at least I would be when normal people addressed me as a grownup. But was it more than that? Did they see into the guts of me? Did the see the lock-picker, wall-piercer, escape artist I imagined becoming? Did they see my inner lust as I stared at Anabelle's tits through her choir robe? I wasn't going to be drinking down any potion in science class after school, but did they see beyond my "163", my good little boy "genius", my "inward vivacity that promises much"? Did they see that it might lead to becoming the mean crook and shyster that I am? Was? Did they see that Mr. Hyde would become far richer than all of them?

At that moment, in my 12-year old wisdom, I decided that since it was obvious to all that I was "Mister Hy-yde", I might as well get good at it. No involuntary metamorphoses for me. I was going to Hyde it up, and stay there. The simple and diabolical mind of a child.

The bookish child became a bookish youth.

I thought poetry would be important, since I would need to come on as suave as tuxedoed Houdini or Dr. Jekyll to get where I planned to go. I started by asking Father Mulvaney what his favorite poems were. He named two, and then required that I go to the library and look them up, and then memorize them, and that he would hear me recite them on Friday (two days away). That was typical of the Jesuits teaching the upper grades.

Without telling Aunt Betsy, I walked down to the big library on Broadway after school, and the nice librarian found the two poems for me, and no doubt thought I was a precocious little angel. Little did she know the devious Houdini purposes behind my research.

I liked very much the rough beast slouching his way to be born. I thought William Butler Yeats really understood my inner Hyde, the Mr. Hyde one, but I was a little afraid that if I recited it too well, Father Gregory would see right into my carefully-to-be-hidden scheme. The dappled things one was too hard to memorize, but it was nice, too, though I had to look up what "dappled" meant. Actually, half the words. Still, my Hydeish plans were original, spare, and strange, so I felt it, too, related to me.

My career as a reader had begun, and not having much money, I figured out a way to steal from the library by putting two books down my pants while I checked out one on the principle that every lie must contain a particle of truth — which at the time, I believed I had invented.

As Ogden Nash later wrote,

There is only one way to achieve happiness on this terrestrial ball,
And that is to have either a clear conscience or none at all.

I imagined at the time that I was simultaneously practicing both. And I was happy — until after a year of collecting, Aunt

Betsy asked me where all those books were coming from. I proudly displayed my library card. She saw the checkout cards were still in their envelopes, and made me bring them all back. Shades of Juicy Fruit. Fortunately, the nice librarian was off that day. The library would be happy just to have the books anonymously back. I even shelved them.

My reading continued apace: The real Stevenson Dr. J and Mr. H — without slutty girls, just old British men. Oh, Mamoulian, you sly one. Sherlock Holmes, of course, and the whole Tarzan series, and most of Dickens which Aunt Betsy owned but never opened. By the time I was fifteen, I had read *Crime and Punishment*, which then turned out to be such a profitable project for me, one from which I fed my book-buying habit. *Portrait of the Artist as a Young Man*, which reminded me of the reality of Hell awaiting me, a vision which I had spent several years trying to forget, and to which forgetting I would have to return. I even read some of the most recent books, kept on a special shelf in the library lobby: *The Trial*, *Steppenwolf*, *The Maltese Falcon*, *Sanctuary*, *Brave New World*, *It Can't Happen Here*, *Murder in the Cathedral*.

Who were my heroes? Moriarity, Raskolnikov, Steerforth, Ivan K, Joseph K, Gatsby, Popeye, Kasper Gutman. A morally mixed bag, but far more interesting than the powers they confronted. And of course, Mr. Hyde. Free at last.

But not as free as transiting from St. Michael's Archangel Elementary to Eastside High School, "Home of the Mighty

Ghosts". Even now, I contribute semi-annually to the EHS Alumni Association, motto: "Once a Ghost, Always a Ghost."

From the Holy Ghost to the Mighty Ghost might not seem like a big jailbreak for a Houdini-ist, but believe me — getting out from under the nuns' robes (though I rarely thought about what was under nuns' robes especially because I was so grossed out that they were bald under their wimples) and away from priestly collaring, left me free as a thought that ye canna confine, as Aunt Betsy used to say.

Even though a Mighty Ghost, I was still too short to join the basketball team, our one big-time varsity sport. But my general peppiness and ferocity, led me to create an alternative cheerleader squad, consisting of myself and two other male intellectuals, for our one appearance at a Ghost game.

One cheer at halftime, and we were excommunicated.

Rah, rah, sis boom bah

Kick 'em in the bollocks, ha, ha, ha!

("Bollocks" being an old Hiberno euphemism for I wasn't sure exactly what.)

No, in fact, I wasn't one of the sporting types and couldn't even pass as one. My escape from Irish-Catholic parochialism led me, in a Hegelian leap (of which, more later), into a devoted atheism.

Remember the first commandment? If Christians were supposed to worship only God, then why were they worshipping statues? Looked like idolatry to me. Maybe the statues were all there was left of God who had skedaddled a long time ago. Maybe there was no God anymore, He had made a cameo appearance, and gone back to sulk wherever else He lived.

I did an experiment. I dared Him to strike me down, at least temporarily, so I could get up again and realize I had been struck down and realize there was a God showing me there was a God by striking me down. He didn't do it. Then I gave him five minutes. Still nothing. Then, because of all my years of Jesuit education, I gave him a whole week. By the end, healthy as ever. A few sniffles, maybe, but hardly in the struck-down category. Maybe I should have said "Strike me dead", since "down" was relative, and dead would at least be clear. But I felt bad about changing the rules in the middle of the game, and beside I was a little afraid of going too far, so I left it at that, and decided there was no God. Since then I have read Nietzsche.

If there was no God, if there was no God… you know, it's Free at last! If God does not exist, as Dostoevsky once whispered to me in my bedroom one fine ninth-grade evening, then everything is permitted. If there is no God, then there are no rules to live by, no moral law we must follow; we (you) can do whatever we (you) (I) want. No hell, no purgatory, no punishment to worry about, no confession to avoid it. No more Holy Days of Obligation. Free at last! Now I could be free to think without guilt about other things, new things, guiltier things. Like Annabelle's you-know-whats and girls in general. It made a big difference to my adolescence.

The passion in the swimming pool would have been impossible without it, especially if God had been checking out the bulge in my swim trunks. And without that Free At Last epiphany, I would never have remembered Houdini, or imagined my future career as shyster.

Though free at last to do so, I came to girls through an indirect route. My first reaction to godlessness was to withdraw into myself and prepare. Prepare for what, I didn't know. Just *reculer pour mieux sauter*. But soon I found my own exclusive company surprisingly boring. Only humans can get bored. What an evolutionary accomplishment! But the beast of boredom does push one toward other things. I was not made to be a good-for-nothing. I would be good for something. I had to confront the actualities of the world.

But seriousness of purpose is potentially dangerous. I sought safety in books until I was ready for the *terra incognita* out there.

Time out:

"Hold on," I've already heard you saying, "What's with all these foreign languages, the Latin or Greek or whatever they are? I don't talk dead foreign languages. That's why they're foreign. Come off it and speaka de English."

To which I respond — First of all, what's wrong with *you?* Most of the world speaks foreign languages. You stupid or something? If you don't know a word, go look it up like I do.

And second of all, are you attacking Jesuits? Are you demeaning my Jesuit education? I didn't get the SMA-E and EHS Latin prizes to sequester all these cultural treasures under a basket. Latin (and Greek, which you'll notice I don't speak) form the building blocks of all Western philosophical thought, and remain foundational to law and medicine, and Latin remains a deep well of Sunday song. You want to be deaf and dumb (*surdum et mutum*)? So go on tawking Noo Joisey.

And third — dead language? Grave, where is thy victory? You don't believe in resurrecting? If God didn't believe in resurrecting, where would you all be now? Worshipping lions and snakes, that's where.

And finally, you don't like my extended, macaronic vocabulary? Who cares? You've already bought this book. Throw it out if you want or feed it to the dog. I've already got my royalty advance.

No foreign language? *O tempora! O mores!* (Cicero)

OK. Forgive the rant, but you brought it on yourselves. Back to what I was saying:

I sought safety in books until I was ready for the *terra incognita* out there. Consequently I became a kind of celebrity at school. A little on the weirdo side, but as the war clouds gathered over Europe, nowhere near as weird as the more global actors. To be honest, I cultivated my weirdness as a kind of student arrogance. So what if I were too short for the basketball team? Was that my fault? No. I, a youth of erudition, would go forth like S.D. "to encounter for the millionth time the reality of experience and to forge in the smithy of my soul the uncreated conscience of my race." That much I could be responsible for.

I made oracular pronouncements like the above, and guess what — girls fell for them, girls — unlike boys — being uniquely susceptible to my sensational management of subordinate clauses.

"What do you wanna be when you grow up?" girls asked, as if looking for a proper potential husband. "A Truth-seeker, I cried, "though the Heavens crush me for apostasy." I would be…"a philosopher"! I left out the "king" part, wary of overreach. I would be an ideologist, which I thought meant someone with a lot of ideas, and having read early Marx, I later amended that, with the abandon of a poet, to the goal of becoming an "ideopraxist", exploring how badness became badness in the worst of all possible worlds.

Needless to say the hoodlums present at my proncuncements (especially the Kong twins and a few other male Jerks from Nowhere) sneered, and in their pathetic nastiness, several times beat me up after school. But that only added to my determination, and made me even more attractive to the motherings instincts of the adolescent girls.

But mothering I did not want. Aunt Betsy's ministrations were quite enough. I wanted sex.

However, sex cost money. Not, of course, in the sub-intellectual manner of red-light districts and hired love. I'm talking about the universal, anthropological ritual of gift giving. Little gifts to those females gifted enough to have gifted me with their beauty and brains and attracted my attention. Which gifts were hard to afford on my now princely allowance of 25¢ a week.

So I spent much time plotting money-making schemes with the new tools that were at my disposal. A chemistry lab, for instance. One of my earliest eleventh grade efforts, a natural result of my life-guard work the previous summer, was Pee & Pay Industries, a limited liability corporation, important because, as the perspicacious reader can easily imagine, I could very well have been sued on many counts.

The idea was to develop a chemical which might be added to public swimming pools nationwide, internationally, which would not only embarrass secret pee-ers, but subject them to fines imposed by the management. A dollar for first offense, five dollars for second, etc. The money would be useful to depression-strapped municipalities, and with enough clever advertising, be attractive even to its victims who, like anyone else, did not relish cavorting in other people's urine. A trail of deep blue or red in a swimmer's wake, or a bloom of color engulfing their standing would be the tipoff. Lifeguards would have more real work, and perhaps even earn their pitiful salaries. There could be bonuses for most tickets written — which would up the alertness level so that lifeguards would not just sit around all day getting woodies over the floating *décolletages*.

Several problems immediately struck me:

1. Toxicity. If I and my employers were to avoid suits, we could not be shown to have provoked skin or lung irritation due to the additive.

2. Concentration. A test tube or even a bucket-full of chemical added to an average size public swimming pool would be diluted at least around a half a million times. So it would have to start out pretty powerful. Another potential source of lawsuits from any affected workers.

3. I understood that this was a good problem to have, but if the project was as successful as I imagined it might be, Pee & Pay would have to amass huge quantities of the key ingredient(s) or the ability to synthesize, process, contain, package, and distribute them or it worldwide.

But first, to mix the chemicals. (I recognized the wonderfully recursive Hydeism in this quest.)

The old high-school chemistry standby: phenolphthalein, that marvelous, if superficial trickster used to convince recalcitrant students that chemistry is fun — which it is not. The useful little guy turns from colorless to pink as a solution turns from acidic to basic. So the question then was what was the pH of urine?

Like the great researchers of the past who risked their lives by ingesting or injecting or constricting or slicing themselves to advance science, I decided to steal some pH paper and a color comparison chart for a week of exacting experiments on my own urinary output.

Initial results were frustrating. My urine pH hovered around 6 — slightly acidic — and phenolphthalein was colorless short of pH 7. I checked different times of day, and noted carefully my food and drink pre-urination. It was clear phenolphthalein would not be the holy grail.

What then? Necessity is the mother of invention. I came up with a plan which would save me time, trouble and expense, thereby sending more profits directly my way. And in a flash, it solved all the three grand problems listed above. Why play junior scientist when I could exercise my inner Houdini? Showmanship and gullibility at play. Even the corporate name could stay the same, "Pee" in this adventure a stand-in for Placebo, a classical character in the great play of medical science. Where would "controls" be, *sans* placebos? And not just medicine was involved, but literature. Was the whole genre of imaginative writing to be dismissed by the bourgeois moral judgments of the herd? Should Wisdom bow to the dwarf of Truth?

In short, and for all the excellent reasons above, I thought I might practice a teenie, venial hoax with a bit of deterrent fiction. I would fill a box of screwtop tubes with colored water (red dye #2 from Aunt Betsy's cabinet), have official stick-on labels printed — Pee & Pay Urine Detector, Proprietary Formula #3 — and sell them to pool directors, along with sets of large, fiercely-lettered signs:

ATTENTION: THE WATER IN THIS POOL CONTAINS A URINE-DETECTING AGENT. AVOID EMBARRASSMENT AND SIGNIFICANT FINES. NO PEEING IN THE POOL!!

Perhaps there would be a graphic illustration, though I'd have to proceed carefully with that.

So — an initial box of six tubes to be used weekly, plus six large signs to decorate the pool perimeter — the complete kit for only $10. That would be less than a quarter a day for health protection for hundreds of patrons.

And look, let's get into moral philosophy and ideopraxis here: even if the tubes contained a placebo, the posted signs themselves would effect a drop in the urine concentration. Never underestimate the massses' penchant to bow to the authority of signage, especially when punishment is threatened. The pool would be cleaner, even if by the pee of one threatened little girl. I would make some money for effecting this improvement. What's to blame? The pool manager could even advertise a urine-free pool, and increase admissions far beyond the 25¢ a day he'd spend for the service. And I'd allow him to keep the six signs — which we know are guaranteed to be effective — even if he unsubscribed from the service.

With this plan I figured my profit margin would be between 700 and 1000%. Not bad for a beginner, and plenty of money to flash at chosen girls.

I began with Augi Mancuso, my boss at Sunnyside. A little doubtful of the chemistry skills of a skinny teenager, nevertheless even that aging dago thought the intent was a worthy one, and proposed taking home a tube to test in his bathtub. I countered that the proprietary chemical was formulated to work under the chemical conditions of a chlorinated pool, and that the test should be made at Sunnyside after the pool had been cleared at closing time. Since it was already late afternoon, I hung around after my shift was up, and shyly ogled batherettes from a shady corner while figuring my next move. I knew what the results of the test would be, and I had to be ready with a convincing rationalization.

At 5:30, Augi drank a couple of beers from the office icebox. At 6, he jumped into the pool, ready for dewatering. "OK, done?" he queried. "How long does it take to turn color?" "What did you have for lunch," I asked? "A couple hot dogs from Beansie's" (the cart outside the pool), says he. "Oh! That explains it," sez I. "The nitrites in hot dogs counter the chemical reaction, so unfortunately it won't turn if you've had hot dogs within the last 24 hours." But that's probably 90% of the kids in the pool.

I had painted myself into a corner with my exculpatory improvisation, and I figured the jig was up. So I moved into the neighboring territory of just-between-us. "Look," I explained, "the point is to get people to stop peeing in the pool, right? Right. The signs will reduce the peeing. Likely? Likely. So don't worry about whether the stuff works or not, the signs will do it whether they've had hot dogs or not." Then, in an excess of confidentiality, "In fact, the stuff is just colored water. It can't work. But the signs are worth ten bucks, don't you think? Even if they don't quite tell the truth?" What he replied struck me like a bolt of lightning.

"It might work," Augi said, "but I'm a Catholic. I cannot tell a lie."

(This is a kind of Catholicism unknown to the crumbling faith of Protestant America under Eisenhower, and now Johnson. How many Catholics does it take to change a light bulb? None. We use candles only.)

All I could manage was 'OK, thanks anyway,' and that conversation careened for the rest of the day, night, week, echoing again and again in my conscience chamber, like the most persistent tinnitus or tune. You can understand why it so shook me up with its sequelae of guilt, confusion, arrogance, certainty, and doubt.

You can also see why I've gone into this incident in such detail, for it captures so much of my early life: my brilliance, my ambition, my as-yet-unmet needs, my fallenness, my pioneering instinct, my Hegelian sublation via Concepts, my horned thoughts, my embrace of Confucius's Doctrine of the Mean.

However, the money-for-sex, or at least the money-for-gifts-for-girls-and-then-sex, problem remained. But that brings my *confessiones* to a major, dominating *leitmotif*: the car.

But before that, and to justify my pool-pissing and future undertakings, a little explanation:

FIRST ANALYTICAL INVECTIVE

Our society is generally engaged in a widespread flight from truth-seeking. Are most people stupid? Well, yes. And ignorance, there is that. Also willful ignorance. All this will remain with us until at least doomsday. We dig fallout shelters, and hire Joe McCarthy to sweep Commies out from under the bed, and sing along to the example of Bert, the animated TV turtle:

When danger threatened him he never got hurt
He knew just what to do
He'd duck and cover, duck and cover,
He'd hide his head and tail and four little feet
He'd duck and cover, duck and cover!
Like you and you and you.

And how better turn our apocalyptic paranoia into popular acceptance of $e=mc^2$, as if to expel its deep horror, than to sell nuclear power as some common household item next to frigidaires, bakelite, and Swedish modern, and label it wholesome, second only to Betty Crocker?

A person like me might very well feel alone in the darkness of our times.

And not our times alone. The devil has modeled all current forms of intellectual tyranny on Plato's *Republic*. Who was the teacher of Nero? Seneca. And who put Alexander of Macedon through his paces? Aristotle. So what does that tell you?

My plan for doing well by doing good irrespective of

so-called Truth reflects the only truly beneficent aspect of the *bellum omnium contra omnes*. Even Kant would approve. To the small-minded, I am simply being dishonest. Yet bearing in mind the Categorical Imperative, my maxim would be "Let small-minded honesty be abolished!" I want others to do likewise, hence there will be no small-minded honesty and ultimately no dishonesty. Hence, as a swindler, I bring about the abolition of swindling. Categorical Imperative applied. The General Good achieved. On the other hand, at some level, everybody is a swindler, so I am doing no more than acting out the democratic ideals of the herd. Thus, appeasement.

Modern man is a container for a mess of pottage, a huge number of indigestible ideological, undigested myths which glop around inside him and create a curious impression of an inside with no corresponding outside, or an outside completely out of touch with its inside. Inside: loftiness, unfathomable depths, mystery. Outside: I'll have a burger, hold the mustard, with a coke and fries. This, of course, is a moral scandal.

Our culture's general embrace of unscrupulousity on the grand scale has given rise to a whole culture of denial, excuse and unconcern. The conscience has been sent off on mandatory, unpaid vacation. And so we swim in an ocean of junk and proliferating debris, and who is to say that into this sea of collective insouciance I should not be able to dip an oar?

Why be ashamed of my noblest acts? A trickster is an architect of worlds. But for Evil, there would be no Good.

But back to cars, the light and darkness of my life. Girls and cars, both.

3. GIRLS AND CARS

Cars made their blessed way into my life when I was sweet fifteen, a Charlie Hyde of the singing heart, an FDR of virtue. The one thing I didn't like about them was the fad of car chicken, an activity that is so stupid, pointless and predictably destructive, that the best thing that can be said about it is that it often does humanity a great service by removing certain characters from the human gene pool. On the other hand, it smashes up some beautiful cars. Car chicken aside, auto bodies were the cocoons in which pupae like myself could mature into forms more sexually adult.

My sixteenth year was sweetly spent in the back seats of Detroit's pleasure machines. No more baby-sitting. The threat was now the possibility of baby-making. But we had our ways, not all of them guaranteed, not all of them honest. Several young women had to go visit relatives out of town for a while, none, I believe, related to me or mine. Even in my inexperience, I understood that it is advisable to be honest, at least in smaller matters. It was Kant, I believe, who said that each should act so that his behavior could be a guiding principle for everyone. Producing unexpected babies, like car chicken, might be seen as good for the human species, but I felt that the small sacrifices I had to make would keep the local female population from shrinking, and so served a greater good.

I remained perfectionist and fierce of spirit, and at a certain point in my Nietzsche studies, I realized I could posit the laws of my own action, beyond any traditional morality. In protest against the wretchedness of reality, free, fearless, immoderate, I simply stepped aside from friends and acquaintances.

It is lonely at the heights. Not everyone liked having to strain their necks looking up at me. While it was inevitable that I could be only tolerated, my firm tone, my healthy human understanding, my correct opinions and pointed mockery did inspire respect. If anyone occasionally shows a gentle temperament, then, as it is said in that wonderful French expression, *au fond*, he is a good fellow, and that his goodness *au fond* can excuse everything else he does, no matter how dishonest.

To be clear — and why be otherwise? — when I was fifteen, I didn't own a car. I was too young in the eyes of the bourgeoisie for one. And I didn't have three or four hundred dollars to buy one. But my friends had cars (this, while I still had friends). And they thought I was cute in a worrisome sort of way, so they invited me along, one, two or even three years their junior. I mean in physical development, and sexual *savoir faire*.

The cars of the early thirties were terrific. What flair, what style, what experimental verve. And I knew every one of them, every make, every model with its specs to four decimal places. And not just Fords, Chevys, and Dodges, Oldsmobiles, Chryslers and Cadillacs, but DeSotos, Lincolns, Nashes, LaSalles, Chandlers, Cords, Hupmobiles, Franklins, Auburns, Hudsons, Packards, Lafayettes, Studebakers…Of course, my friends could afford only used cars and hand-me-downs, cars from the 20s and even before, some with hand cranks.

Liam Shaughnessy had access to my favorite car of all, a perky '29 Ford Model A Roadster — with a rumble seat. Really heavy loving usually took place in the back seats of touring cars, but this little jobbie, the classiest car I'd ever seen, forest green with red upholstery and red wire wheels, had only two up front and the rumble. So Liam and his current victim were up there, inside, while I and mine were out back, romantic, under the stars, doing our doings basically in public. Which was generally ok, since I was younger, and my role was to take out the kid sisters of the real girls up front. Sometimes mine didn't even have titties. But they were excited to go out with an intellectual, their deluded parents were satisfied that the girls were mutually chaperoning, and we'd always come back on time, but with enough time to get things accomplished. Liam always scored, at least he said so, and the rocking of the car and the moaning of its inhabitants would seem to confirm it. But back in the rumble, being public, it was much more Platonic, to the point of being early Cotton Mather, our doings developing in contrast to the turbulence up in the cockpit. But more than once, little sis shed frightened tears over what she had gotten herself into.

All in all, I'd have to say that I soon got tired of my role of babysitter cum possible future beau. The stars were nice, the wind in our hair, the fact that you could take your date's hand helping her up to the step plate on the rear fender, and into the seat beside you. But more than that — rocking and groaning, etc. — that just couldn't be. Even I knew that. I was forced to engage in charming, intelligent talk about puerile subjects, just to keep the whole thing from being embarrassing. An entertainer I was, a real lover not. At least not then, at 15, in Liam's rumble seat.

More attractive than the girls was the car itself, and the new hero that came with it.

No, it was not Henry Ford, he of the old Tin Lizzie, he of the "car for the great multitudes" which you can have in any color you like, "as long as it's black", he, who I admit had created the car culture which has formed and ennobled my life, that aging and cantankerous semi-buffoon of anti-labor and antisemitic fame, the nasty, eccentric gaunt gray ghost who thought the model T was as much car as regular Americans needed — it was not Henry Ford the First who was my new hero, but his much maligned genius son, the great unsung Edsel Ford.

No son-of-the-old-codger he. And of course the old codger hated him as only a father can hate a son. Drove

Edsel to an ulcerous, early death, did his pop, and along the way took every occasion to publicly humiliate and insult him.

Since I will never allow anyone to punch me in the stomach, and will never offer up my gastro-intestines to be brutalized or diminished by fatherly others, so I must value my heroes' faults, tragic and fatal. From their mistakes I have learned.

But what of their achievements? From these I must take advantage. Even now, my abdominals are hard, and even now I worship and glorify Edsel's redesign of the tin-lizzie, the sweet Model A — "A" for the start of a whole new line, a new verve-and-dash approach to automotive styling and safety. Not to mention the rumbleseat. Go, Edsel, go!

With the end of Prohibition, hooch was actually harder to get than before, especially in the neighborhood. A lot of families had come from County Sligo, where making booze was everybody's business. They brought their habits, and their stills over with them. When times got hard, they just brewed more, some opened establishments on the first floor (peephole door required), and of course some of their best customers were cops and local pols.

We kids knew all about alcohol, how to make it, where it was stashed — we got into places, dontcha know. Without prohibition, the big guys took over and drove moms and pops out of business. But several of my friends kept small home stills going if only to soup up the car rides. The Model Ts had a top speed of 40 miles per hour, and a car had to be in pretty good shape to get that. So driving our pocket flasks around was not so dangerous. But Edsel's snazzy Model A's could routinely make 65 miles per hour — a big difference. People started to get killed on the roads, and not just drunks. And Model A owners were themselves a bit jazzier, more devil-may-care. So even with windshield wipers standard, safety glass windshields, and four wheel brakes, mortality was up. But when did mortality ever stop an American?

Yes, the sex got better when I graduated from bumper seat to sedan rears, and even classier when I got my own used Chevy at 18, but not so much better or classier that it eclipsed the greater beauties, the enablers and containers, the chariots of us newish gods, the sensational cars.

Until…

I first spied Deirdre through squinted eyes from the height of my chair, when she emerged from the women's showers at the far end of the pool. At that moment, I was without a disabling erection, so I stood up the better to see and be seen. I should have blown my whistle, but I was so gob-smacked I didn't think of it.

She was heartstoppingly, fatally, lovely, I thought, even though I felt my heart beating faster, not slower — but fast enough that it might certainly stop. She glided, Circe-like, from the locker room exit to the steps on the shallow end, descended the three steps into the water (Marcel Duchamp,

think again!), and stood there considering her options —
not one of which seemed to be me. Though below the
waist she was optically foreshortened like a chondroplastic
dwarf, what was left above was so stunning as to make the
other girls in her vicinity look like carp or toads or bloated
manatees. Atop her long, lovely neck, — supported by at
least eight or nine vertebrae, a neck you just wanted to bite
— atop that neck, a head so small and lovely it seemed to
float into the sky all on its own. Up, up, up. What posture!
That sweet oval sitting weightlessly atop the sinuous vertical
of her spine. The cliché princess would have been blond,
streaming golden strands, halfway down her back. But this
one must be a flapper's child, perhaps, a bobbed child, with
red-brown bangs and sides framing her cheeks, almost
meeting under her chin, leaving her neck exposed, the better
to bite you, my dear. She immersed her body, then swam,
undine, right over to me, and paused, with her arms on the
rim of the pool a single yard below my feet.

At the same time I felt that she was completely unaware
of me, hovering intensely three feet above her. How could
that be? Aren't humans supposed to be sensitive to the great
power of Love?

Was this real? Did I dream her trajectory? Look at those
limbs propped below me, undulant, erotic. She was perfect,
thin but amply boobed, and that face, that face, my heart went
out to that face. So soft it was, so demure, as if she didn't even
imagine that she was pretty.

At the same time I felt that she was completely unaware
of me, hovering intensely three feet above her. How could
that be? Aren't humans supposed to be sensitive to the great
power of Love?

Love, yes, love, that partial insanity! This was no mere Lust, as it had been so often before, an emotion that would have been satisfied with a quick rescue, my arm reassuringly across some lovely's chest, her darling head pressed against my neck, Charlie Hyde tugging the grateful victim to poolside, my hero! (It never happened, but you can't just sit there all day hoping for a threat to someone else's life.) I knew it was love because welling up, unbidden, from my deepest depths was no Bach cantata, or Monteverdi madrigal, or even some erotic Elizabethan ditty, but a Gershwin song I'd heard last year at the movies, "Love Walked Right In". Yes, Ira, yes, one magic moment and my heart seemed to know…that Love said hello — Love, not Lust, mind you — though not a word was spoken.

So why didn't she hear the same tune when it was sounding full blast not five feet above her head? Was she deaf? Should I scream the lyrics at her? Blow my whistle? What if she had a low startle threshold?

I leaned over and said, as calmly as I could, "Can I help you, Miss?" She looked up wonderingly, and brought me into focus. "Oh…no thank you, I was just thinking about something." And off she swam, her lovely upper back and shoulders gleaming wet in the sun.

Our first words, our first dialogue. Our first pillow talk, had there been a pillow. "OK," I mumbled.

But the reply was disturbing. *What* was she thinking about? She comes to a public pool to cool off and have fun, and she stops swimming after maybe 25 feet, to pause and think. This could be ominous for me. A boyfriend, surely. How could it be otherwise?

I had to see her again, and somehow find out. But how? She had swum away to the other side of mid-pool, probably to get away from pushy lifeguards, and be able to think about him, him!, in peace and quiet. Or as quiet as it could get in the maniacal screaming ambiance of a public pool. Clearly I couldn't pester her again while she was swimming and I on duty. Would she get up on the diving board? That would be something, possibly beyond my ability to endure.

But why hadn't I ever seen that angelic image before? Over the three summers I'd been at Sunnyside, surely I would have noticed her. She didn't go to Eastside High, that was certain. Was she perhaps from out of town, visiting a cousin, or worse? Why was she alone? Where were her friends?

August '39 was the summer of my junior year. My desire endured unquenched. Everyone seemed worried about Hitler, but I was worried about never seeing her again. And I was even *more* worried about seeing her again and dealing with the boundless anguish people can inflict on one another. And that's exactly what was inflicted on me: when school started, there she was in my home room class.

Mr. Minster introduced the two new students. One was some eyebrowless hulk, unquestionably a moron, whose name I forget. The other was…Deirdre Dunnigan, a transfer student from Bridgeport, Connecticut. So that's why she wasn't already surrounded by girlfriends piggybacking on her beauty, or pimply-faced ruffians, lusting to smear their secretions all over her. But at that moment, her coming out, t-zero, the clock started ticking, the starting pistol was fired, the flag went down, and all hell would break loose around her I was sure. She needed protection, and I would be her protector. But I'd have to figure out how to get to her through the pack which would surround her at the next class break.

One thing I hadn't counted on: beauty makes one shy, and I was not the only observer so intimidated. Strange as it may seem, in her first month as the new beauty on campus, she was always surrounded by a bubble of empty space which cleared the world around her like a 300 pound line blocker. As she glided angelically down crowded halls between classes, people would step aside to preserve her circumference at $2\pi r$, where $r=4$ feet or so, a true anomaly in a 12 foot wide corridor. Heads turned as she went by, not angrily as if she smelled bad (she didn't), but with a kind of "What was that??" admiration, a sense of having been briefly graced.

So my competition was basically with myself, at least at the beginning.

How to start, how to begin? Clearly, my "Can I help you, Miss?" didn't bring forth from her a testimony of love. Perhaps she was a grammatical purist, and I should have said "May I". Unlikely. And outside our original roles of life-guard and potential drownee, an offer to help would be confusing, at best.

Pondering the issue, I found myself (coincidence?) walking past the chemistry lab, and immediately the thought struck me, a racial memory, as it were, of my literary antecedent, or at least his polar opposite, Dr. Jekyll, with his enlightenment faith in potions. A love potion, why not? I realized the Dr. Jekyll potion attempts did not go all that well, but that was back in the last century, without all the more sophisticated techniques and equipment now available in a high school chemistry lab.

I knew this research project would not be trivial. Aphrodisiacs like Coke + aspirin were well understood by boys in their later teens. But — Aphrodite forgive me — concerning Deirdre, I was not after sex. I was after love, mad love-falling of a courtly kind, lasting a lifetime, and without the side effects of Isolde's — yet another botched job.

I also knew that this research could not be carried on in the EHS chemistry lab, using the available, common reagents. I was not going to subject my love to Hydrochloric or Sulfuric acid, or any of their salts or derivatives. I suspected I'd need to get into some arcane ingredients, wild botanical ones — after consulting the requisite manuscripts. So, under cover of early winter darkness, I borrowed some beakers and flasks, a graduated cylinder, half a dozen pipettes, and a pint of pure ethanol for home tincture extractions. A long Saturday at the Rutgers library gave me, I thought, the hints I needed.

Potions in myth and literature are usually concocted by

witches or fairies, and I was neither. But I had a steady hand, and I was determined. There are no easy occupations.

Many possibilities were proffered in the literature, none of them, I suppose, double-blind tested, but I had to go on instinct here, and also using a recipe with obtainable ingredients. I found one entirely stocked in Aunt Betsy's kitchen. Why not start there?

Instructions were in a 1915 volume of *hexerei*, probably fraudulent, of witchcraft theory and practice. Thus it went:

One handfull of hips of rose

Whose wonders you will now transpose

Aunt Betsy had a box of rose hips tea which I thought would do. The "hips" seemed a bit salacious for this project, and at the same time, not salacious enough, containing little of the rose-smell all women fall for and which another volume claimed created arousal and affection — of which the latter was crucial. So to the tea, I added an equal portion of the popery my aunt kept in a little corked bottle, which looked like it had rose petals. I guess that's what the Pope used to smell good, and if it was good enough for him…

Three silver spoons of golden honey

Made by bees in meadows sunny.

Honey we had, but I suspect that what Auntie called silverware was not pure silver. Three teaspoons into the beaker.

Three silver spoons of finest brandy

This mix, your modus operandi.

Damn, there were those silver spoons again, and if whatever we had didn't measure up, this run would be doubly vexed.

OK, I had the ingredients or reasonable substitutes. Now what? The dried material would have to be rehydrated to regain its glow, so into a stoppered flask they went, and left on my windowsill for sun and moon to act upon. I figured a week would do it. Into the mix, I added the honey and brandy, and just a touch of ethanol to make things more scientific, and less homey. Another week for the tincture extraction, this time in the dark of my closet. Then I poured the mixture through a strainer into a Jekyllesque beaker, and there it was, golden and fragrant.

Before subjecting my darling to it, I thought I'd sample it myself to see if it increased my longing, and did not do me in, though I couldn't see what in the ingredients could be poisonous. I had kept careful lab notes concerning quantities, temperatures, length of day and night, imagining that this would be trial #1 of possibly many.

It didn't taste bad. In fact, it was delicious, sweet and rosaceous, with a slight tang of brandy. I could, in good conscience, slip it to her. Oh, there was a chant to be said over the concoction, more superstition than science, but I said it anyway:

When you upon this drink shall dine,
You shall be mine, you shall be mine.
You shall be mine for ever more,

I didn't see any harm in saying it, so I repeated it six times over the open beaker, then poured off a portion into an empty, well-washed bottle of nose drops. I planned to slip a few drops onto her mashed potatoes or into her cup of soda when next I could accost her in the cafeteria.

But I couldn't just hit and run because, at least according to common superstition, I had to be the first person she would set eyes on after ingesting, or God knows who she could fall in love with, piggybacking on my potion.

While the other boys were still frightened of her beauty, by the time it was time to try the potion, she had already acquired several relatively ugly girl followers. It is strange how few truly good faces there are in the world if you really think about it. Hers was one.

I had often noticed how the better looking girls seemed to pair up with ugly best friends, perhaps for protection from male onslaught, in some cases (but not Deirdre's) for narcissistic comparison. For the homely girl, the advantage is clear — a ticket into coed society with a frisson of vicarious romance.

Two of the hangers-on were chatting with her at the table, sitting on either side. There was no way I could get near enough with my medicine dropper since leaning all the way across the table, dropper in hand would never do. But I had also noticed a secondary phenomenon in the relationship between beauties and their beasts: whenever a handsome young prince would approach, the uglies would withdraw into themselves, assuming, usually correctly, that they were not the object of interest, and that dialogue between princess and prince took precedence over whatever had been going on.

Bottle in hand, hidden beneath my lunch tray, I decided to test my theory on the trio at the table. "May I join you?" I asked politely, counting on the dilution of my presence, only 1/4 of the group, instead of an embarrassing one-on-one. "Please," she said, speaking for the trio, and with a graceful gesture, indicated the bench across the way. What a charming voice! An unimaginably lovely smile.

Like clockwork, her two familiars made their ungainly exits, allowing their understanding of the main event to proceed. I palmed the bottle, and with one hand unscrewed the dropper under the table so it could easily be extracted, fully loaded.

Luckily, she had forgotten something she had to say to one of them, excused herself, and hurried out to catch her. Returning to the table after the confabulation, she took a sip of coke, and daintily lifted a forkful of coleslaw to her perfect lips. Both coke and coleslaw had been spiked, and in the interval of her absence, I had intoned, sotto voce and very quickly

When you upon these drops shall dine,

You shall be mine, you shall be mine.

You shall be mine for ever more…

And then she returned.

I began with the only hook I had: "Say, were you at the Sunnyside pool the end of last summer?"

"Why yes," she said, and brightened up, as if the sun could become more radiant still.

It worked! It worked! First try, it worked! O, Jekyll, O Hyde, O Lavoisier and Mendeleev! I could hear the thud as she fell in love.

I told her I remembered her, and she thought that amazing(!) I asked if she were new in town, and she told me the story of her family's recent immigration to Paterson. I must have been the first male to dare my way into her boy-terrorizing bubble. Walking through walls I was, as it was foretold. Mind-forged manacles, away! An ex-Catholic saved by popery and witchcraft.

4. LOVE AND MARRIAGE

It was a surprise to discover that perhaps she, so discreet, so comely, was not all that bright. But her vagueness added even more to her allure. More and more to discover. And if she was a goody-goody —well, I was a baddie-baddie, and all the better: opposites attract and complement one another, yin and yang. And since I, the evil yin, did have a generative dot of goodie-goodieness left over from my altar boy days, it was very likely that she, too, as do all created beings, had within her that as yet undiscovered yin dot of wild abandon. Ain't we got fun?

We would go out, and I would do most of the talking. She would fix me in her gaze, absorbedly, like a child. Those clear features, lovely cheekbones, perfect nose, and the sheen and smell of the red-brown hair caressing her face, that face. What defines a beautiful girl? She. Over and over she, she, she. She looked like a blushing queen. Those limpid eyes. Even her feet were beautiful.

She didn't read much, as far as I could tell, but she did devour the daily horoscopes in the Star-Ledger. She told me I was a Scorpio, which didn't sound very nice, even if it seemed appropriate: intense, powerful, profound, passionate, fiercely independent. It didn't sound very nice until she told me she was a Virgo (as if I couldn't tell, though I was worried), and Virgos and Scorpio made the best pairs. Shocking, it was. I looked it up: deep love, sexual compatibility, an intense karmic bond. I was for that.

But karmic bond or no, I couldn't imagine actually doing it — it — with my delicate, demure Deirdre, making it — intensely, passionately, powerfully. I wouldn't want to shatter her, disrupt her moon on the water. I was even worried about messing up her beautiful hair. Her curse of beauty.

I thought about breaking out in song, just to shake her up a little. Not a Schubert lied, but something more like "Hey good lookin', whatcha got cookin'?" But what if she criticized my pronunciation? In '39, I did have access to a hot rod Ford and a two-dollar bill, if I hadn't spent it. "Hey, sweet baby, don'tcha think maybe…we could find us a brand new recipeee?"

But I didn't. I took it slow. Low idle. We went to church together to listen to the music. I was not struck down. I met her parents, very briefly. Most polite, how do you do, Mr. Dunnigan, Mrs. Dunnigan? I'm fine, how are you? I already hated them.

After two months, I was invited to dinner.

It all became obvious. Edward Dunnigan was part of some kind of Irish mafia, sent up north to capo a Jersey division of something or other. I don't know what — diamonds, liquor, gambling, protection. Whatever it was it wasn't obvious in the normal well-appointed milieu of an upper-middle class house in a relatively posh area of north Paterson. Mama and the girls were in the kitchen, while the big man grilled me on my credentials: was I a rapist or a potential son-in-law, or at worst, both? Was there a possible future for me in his shadowy organization? He never mentioned any of this, but I could tell from his eyes what he was sniffing at.

If you want to know what God thinks of money, all you have to do is consider the rich. Here was a man, basically normal looking, a bit on the short side, but trim, even delicate like Deirdre, whose reddish Celtic face was slightly marred by crooked teeth. Consequently, he didn't smile much. But with his silvered reddish hair, and upscale demeanor, he would pass for an important person, or at least someone posing as an important person. Even without one, he looked like he was smoking a cigar.

The old phrenologists had noticed the sign of an "organ of destructiveness", often visible in surgeons and butchers as a bulge above the ears. My future potential father-in-law showed it in spades — both sides. It portended a "capacity to inflict pain without compunction." On the other hand, those chromosomes had produced the heavenly D. But on the first hand again, his colorless blue eyes and pomaded head announced grasping, greedy, cunning calculation, so I had to watch my step.

We men sat in the living room, I on the French Provincial couch, he in a deep red leather smoking chair. His remarks about his daughters, whom he referred to only as a group, the way one might talk about the Pleiades or the Andrews Sisters, were effectively non-committal as to their wonders. I accept as a fact that usually parents do "love" their children — Darwinian reasoning here is too obvious to ignore. But as for Mr. Dunnigan's actually "liking" them — or his wife — enjoying them as people — that wasn't so clear. His mind seemed armed against all emotional assaults. He appeared cold-blooded, a snake of sorts, perhaps one of the tribe expatriated by Patrick, a homier new world version of evil.

When dinner was called, I was reminded of the old adage, "If you're not at the table, you may be on the menu." Eat, or be eaten. We walked into the dining room. I'll never forget what I saw.

Caitlin and Kaylin, Deirdre and Claire, a supreme celebration of nubility — the collected beauty was too dazzling to completely take in. My own dear darling occupied no more than one-quarter of the splendor. My heart expanded: I was instantly in love with all of them. I saw my future children emerging from all four wombs. I could have impregnated them all that evening, right and left, and their mother too, and perhaps even their father. And all the women at least seemed to love me, and I in turn looked into all their eyes with passion.

Deirdre was third down the line, with two elder and one younger sister, none of them too old or too young to ravish. And Antoinette, her gauloise mama, wasn't too bad either, obviously an ex-flapper of unextinguished, mischievous spirit. Ooo, la, la, them there eyes!

But here before me at the dinner table, along with the pot roast and beaujolais, was the opportunity to take control, to focus my desires on my desire, once unique, but now served up generic, for the demon Dunnigan chromosomes to have and to hold, and hopefully to propagate into the world, a world so commonly lacking in beauty.

I had started out with Deirdre, so, in spite of the treasures at the table, to Deirdre I was linked. What faithful sister would accept my wooing glance? None. What parent would try to wrest a lover away from her child like Fyodor K? Not in this house. The route was set. The travelers, Deirdre Dunnigan and Charles Hyde.

It was just after the start of the war which we all had known was coming. Late autumn '39. I was now of age to be drafted. And so, my destination — most desired, but also most useful: the altar of potentially draft-deferring marriage.

For all her being descended from the testicles of a probable serpent, my fiancée was a perfect girl. A bit ornamental, but still, she stood for health, fidelity, true love, bliss. Between right and wrong, she clung to right. For me, this was romance: believing the unbelievable.

We had two weddings, the first, when I took her hand as my EHS prom queen, and we promenaded together in the crazed kaleidoscope of mirror ball lighting and popping of flash bulbs as we took our thrones in the school gymnasium. King and Queen of the Mighty Ghosts we were, a title at once triumphant, hubristic, and damned.

The second wedding was the "real" one, the wedding for the parents and their country club friends, the catered wedding with the $5,000 wedding dress and the professional band. The priest spoke his gorgeous Latin rigamarole in the name of Christ. With the help of St. Paul, who despised marriage, I swore to cherish her till death do us part, no matter what. In church, the organist played Wagner the Nazi and Mendelssohn the Jew. At the reception the band played "In the Mood". And boy, was I in the mood for our first wedded night.

The inquisitive and no doubt foul-minded reader will be curious as to how it went, how a virgin unspotted might fare under the weight and guidance of Charles the Bold, a sexually savvy maneuverer like myself. I, too, would like to know. Perhaps there is something beyond maneuvering. We shall see. Hang on.

Full of religion, or at least of religiosity, I was neverthe-less — and still am — propelled by fact, logic, and critical thinking. I can truthfully say how it was for me.

I begin with some simple, axiomatic, observations:

— I was a human being, born of human parents, though they are both human no longer.

— I had two eyes, two ears, a mouth and four hands and feet.

— I had many good teeth, and this was before the days of widespread fluoridation.

— I felt myself, and was seen by others, as criminally handsome.

Even so, try as I might to be otherwise, I was basically a good kid. I was idealistic, wearing my heart on my swim trunks and sleeve. I may have even been a half-saint type, an angel, if a sinful one, as demonstrated by my love of church music. Mine was a tender heart, often sclerotic, but full of love nonetheless.

These were the basic ingredients of my wedding night.

So how did it go? Well, the wish is father to the event, and my wishing is an act of extreme emotional intensity. I wish the way some others feel. To me, poetry consists of standing up and saying with no concealment whatsoever, what it is to be conscious, on earth, in the moment. And in that moment, morality seemed interesting but not too gripping, reasonable but not inspiring, fun but without enough tragedy. Mind you, I was not into doing anything idiotic. Nevertheless, since misunderstanding, loneliness, and inarticulateness are virtually root conditions, it didn't go all that well. When I asked the classic Socratic question, "How was it for you?", she responded, "OK." She was very beautiful.

It was the forties, the fabulous forties-to-be, the late summer of 1940 to be exact. Our new home, given to us as a wedding gift, had been stuffed with the latest large appliances, General Electric thises and Frigidaire thats, all delivered from God knows where in an unmarked truck by taciturn moving men. A non-crookèd house, delivered by the definitely crookèd.

The daughter of a fat cat, and a princess-queen besides, Deirdre did not have to work, and could take some time off after high school. I, on the other hand, had to find a job, be the wage earner, until I had proved myself and earned the right to be taken into the family business, whatever it was.

So charming was our abode, that my young wife rarely left the house, and only when it was absolutely necessary. She filled her days with reading ominous magazines, like LIFE, filled with ominous photographs, in ominous black & white of ominously impending world catastrophe, balanced with ads for more household appliances in color. Pick one.

She also painted — delicate watercolors copied from paintings in expensive art books, which her father miraculously supplied. Her pietas were especially moving, and I wonder now if she was trying to tell me something. She also listened to her (our) 18-tube Stromberg-Carlson art-deco radio. One day, a Steinway spinet arrived unexpectedly at our door. She was so delighted, so excited, that on its very first day she learned to play chopsticks, and by the end of the first week, could bang out a basic accompaniment to "Heart and Soul". Somewhere, Hoagy Carmichael is surely still applauding.

Came the fall, though, and those pictures in LIFE began to resonate in my life as well as hers. On Sept 16, 1940, a day which will live in infamy, goons in the US Congress passed the Selective Service Training and Service Act — the first peacetime conscription in America's history.

I was almost 20. I had reached the age of reason. I was fearless except for death, and an intense fear of appendicitis. Other than that, quite fearless. But I knew that you don't make peace by preparing for war. Somebody said that. All males between 21 and 36 had to register to kill and die for the government, whether they voted for it or not. I was still 20, but my clock was ticking. Something would have to be done. I was certainly not going to leave my productive life as an apprentice mechanic at Dolan's Auto Sales, and my ongoing audition for joining the firm, whatever it was, to head over to Europe to get my ass shot up or killed. I had a new, beautiful wife. She might get lonely, and then what?

I read the classification rules with minute attention. There seemed to be several routes out, given that we had not yet gone to war. I could be a conscientious objector to military service, maybe, if I could prove to the draft board that my life had been based on religious beliefs which prohibited participation in war, and was not confined to any particular war. Well, I had been an altar boy, probably on record somewhere.

I served Father Mulvaney, and mumbled his *Dona Nobis Pacem* weekly for more than a few months.

But asking God for peace, especially if I hadn't believed in Him for at least five years didn't seem all that convincing, even to me. I was president of my own private Nietzsche Club, and the old moustache didn't think too highly of JC. They could probably see how many Nietzsche books I had checked out of the library.

Too tough, too nervous-making to claim a 1-O. I could get a 2-S for as long as I was in college, if I were in college, which I wasn't, and who wanted to go to college anyway, when I needed to be making money, not spending it? I could pretend to be unfit for military service, but that was beneath my dignity, and would be belied by my three years of Red Cross certified life-guarding, and my strong physique. What was left was a 3-A deferment, hardship to dependents.

Deirdre was hardly dependent on me, at least financially. It was if anything the other way round, as I would no doubt be making less than minimum wage, or maybe even paying Dolan to be trained. But maybe the draft board didn't know that, or maybe Ed Dunnigan could swing things with them to keep his son-in-law home and his daughter happy. But what I really needed to cinch things up was kids, enough of them to last through the war.

Fucking obsessively in order to stay out of the military isn't the most romantic way to go about it, but we both knew our duty to ourselves, each other, and our country, and Deirdre was good enough to go along with the plan. By the time I had to register, she was already pregnant, (what would you expect from so beautiful and faithful a young woman?), and I could in good conscience apply for a dependency deferrment. I figured the war would be over soon after we charged in. By the time the generals moved into their new offices in their polygon in Virginia, we ourselves were already five, Deirdre, Cooie, Looie, Dooie, and myself. She just popped them out annually, like clockwork.

But as she did, repeatedly, her supernatural beauty began to fade. The successive glows of pregnancy put out ever less wattage. Her fairyland skin turned to mere silk, and then a finely-woven cotton. She picked up fifteen pounds in each pregnancy, and quickly lost ten between them, and 105 pounds grew to 120. I don't blame her — it's Nature's way with women, of course — but the unfortunate fact is, I don't like fatties. Or rather, I'm capable of liking them, but my desire plummets logarithmically per pound. When younger, I was able to guard an entire swimming pool of pleasingly plump maidens without getting a boner once over the course of two hours. I kept track.

I was concerned about this, but my attention turned sharply in the fall of 1945 to something far more threatening. No, it was not the explosions over Hiroshima and Nagasaki, which, after all, affected northern New Jersey very little.

It was my hair, my movie star hair. It began to fall out. Not immediately, not in great clumps, but each day there were more hangers-on to my brush. A softer brush did not help. At first I thought "Oh, it's just male pattern baldness, a sign that I'm becoming more mature. Like Victor Mature. It will give me more standing with my three little girls, when they become aware of the attractiveness of older men.

But my initial confidence in Nature's way was soon upended. It was clearly beyond male pattern baldness. I was heading toward frank alopecia. How could this happen? My father was not bald or even balding. I thought of him as "the big hairy". Was this finally the great revelation as to how I, so morally compromised, could have emerged from two such saintly parents? Perhaps my mother was not as saintly as she pretended, or perhaps that saintliness was *in remissionem peccatorum*, as Father Mulvaney used to chant. Perhaps their dying together of the flu was further punishment for a crime against the Sixth Commandment. And if she was doing it, my father may have been getting some of his own to pay her back. What else could explain their death duet? None of my friends' parents died.

Useless speculation, the evidential trail grown cold. I had more important things to concern myself with: stopping the retreat of my hair. I approached the problem from both ends, that is to say, from the present forward, and simultaneously consulting histories, medical and otherwise, for possible cures which the medical establishment in its arrogance, and the pharmaceutical industry in its greed, have deemed anathema.

The most obvious experiment, weather permitting, was

to hang for ten minutes a day upside down from a tree branch in our back yard, and to do a daily count of hairs left in the brush — not an inconsiderable pain in the ass. No demonstrable relationship: the fallen hair count increased. Increased blood flow to the scalp, I had thought. Would that not increase oxygenation and nutrient flow? Apparently not — or if it did, the hair kept falling anyway. Neither niacin capsules to create flushing, nor cayenne rubbed into the scalp changed the result. Nor did wrapping my head in scalding towels to draw out the sebum which may have been plugging the follicles.

I hit the Rutgers Library on free evenings. Starting with "Bald", I quickly encountered Charles the Bald, the spectacular ninth century Emperor of the Holy Roman Empire, and possibly even an ancestor of my true father, whoever he was, from before the Norman Invasion. This finding could have been a fluke, a statistical anomaly, and perhaps even a false name, since there were absolutely no portraits of him without his crown. But then I discovered that in his very court lived and sang the great poet and composer Hucbald le Chauve, both bald and *chauve* at the same time. And to top it off, Hucbald, in his chauveness, was the author of the amazing *Ecloga de Calvis*, In Praise of Bald Men, the only known philosophic defense, praise, blessing, and justification of baldness. And furthermore, in this great poem every word of its 146 lines begins with the letter C.

Don't believe me?

Carmina, clarisonae, cantata, Camenae.

Comerae condigno conabor carmina calvos,

Contra cirrosi crines confundere colli…

(For all you illiterati out there:

Muses, sing a boisterous song for bald men.

I will try to adorn bald heads with a fitting song,

And, conversely, to muss the hair of those with ample curls…)

Is that a better opening than the Canterbury Tales or what? This was one serious baldy.

Needless to say, Charles le Chauve became his generous patron. And thank goodness for my Jesuit training, since clearly no translation can do justice to its wonders. I think it likely that I was the only auto mechanic trainee on the eastern seaboard awash in its wonders.

There was admittedly little in it to guide my physiological research. However, in my ninth century rummaging, the praise of baldness notwithstanding, I did come up with several procedures in the pharmacopoeia worth trying. I boiled mustard oil with henna leaves, and rubbed the cooled down oil into my scalp. Nothing. I made a paste from honey, beer, and boiled wheat, and applied it gently to my scalp. Again nothing, but here, perhaps because I was unable to follow the instructions completely. The massage was supposed to be done by the hands of a virgin, and there were no virgins around — at least none that I wanted knowing what was going on — so I did it myself, and I, too, was not a virgin. Who knows?

The Vikings used goose droppings, but there were none I could identify as such in the neighborhood. Cow or pig feces were also recommended, but I couldn't see resorting to that, plus where in Paterson would I get them? There were more remedies tried, ancient and modern. I won't bore you with them since the results were always the same: nada. Alcpecia on the march.

It may not surprise you that catastrophic hair loss in a dashing young man about town is a devastating hit cn his self-esteem, and therefore his libido. I had been the old me for so long that I looked upon each fresh sign of decomposition as treachery. Aging, loss of control, confronting mortality. That, plus my fattening three-children-in-diapers wife was changing the key, color, lighting, and tempo of my world.

The boys at the shop with their sex-driven jests, the cutie calendars on the walls, even the feel of grease on my hands, set self-destructive psychic energies whirling. I was constantly checking mirrors, the side- and rearview mirrors on the cars we worked on, even the telescoping inspection mirrors we used to look at difficult to see engine aspects. Vanity becomes more vain when threatened, and so did I, making sure everything except up top was alway shipshape, more than shipshape, and my selection of hats was snappy and high-end. I particularly liked my work cap, which, though forest green, was a modern-day version of the *bonnet rouge*, connecting me with the spirit of my Irish ancestors during the revolution. That was the kind of spirit you needed for confronting issues of major balding.

And then, a slap in the conceptual face, I began reading about survivors of our atomic attacks, balding, balding everywhere, and the possibility of radiation — invisible, unfeelable, untraceable — began to haunt, with my hair loss, the canary in the New Jersey coal mine.

None of the many advertised creams or medicines seemed to be effective, or why hadn't the problem been definitively solved and capitalized upon? With the correct approach one could become a millionaire, selling to sad sacks and comb-overs. But what if there were a surprise value to our dropping an atom bomb on the Nips? What if the results actually showed us the real cause for hair loss? And what if *I* were to be the one to patent that investigation? I needed to test the hypothesis.

I actually went into Newark and bought a Geiger-Müller counter. Alpha particles, beta particles and gamma rays, and who knows how many other nasty Greek invaders — I'd be on to them, like Hector. A heuristic gift from the Hun and Jap, dealt directly to me to make me rich. And famous. Dr. Hyde's Baldness Cure, no, Baldness Treatment. I thought maybe I should use a pseudonym or an atomic science-related logo.

Counter in hand, and $25 down in purse, I began my investigations. No matter where I stuck my probe, there were no significant results. An occasional tick or two, but I understood the concept of background radiation. Luckily I was able to return the machine before the warrantee week was out. I told them it was broken, and they believed me.

It seemed I would just have to adjust to being a cue ball, an almost-biblical-level charm against vanity. Good, I could be less vain without making any bigger changes. Whether it would affect my relationship with women other than my wife remained to be seen. But I hadn't gotten there yet.

Deirdre, herself, left off her gentle teasing, and — typically — developed some rather lovely new techniques for stroking and petting and calming, diplomatically dealing with the fibrous residue in her hands. In spite of her weight gain, she remained a loving wife.

And I have to admit that 20 years into it, I've gotten to enjoy the Jersey breeze caressing my noodle if I ever take off my hat.

5. FROM WIFE TO LIFE

Deirdre. Deirdre of the Sorrows — my sorrows at any rate. After dinner, varied for five different palates, her beautiful eyes would mist over, her blinks become longer, and, with the girlies put to bed, she too, would soon follow. She, without me, whose mechanics did not include three screaming brats.

I loved to watch them all sleeping together, the young mother-goddess, thickening, perhaps, but still a stunning young woman who in her waking world wanted nothing more than my love, my faithfulness, and to see the little ones grow soundly into the beauties they already promised to be. Four angelic heads snuggled together. Who requires wisdom in sleepers of such design? But would Deirdre remain faithful to her rapidly aging king? She needed testing.

Benny Goodman and his band would be playing at the Savoy on the weekend of our fifth anniversary, and I thought we could celebrate (and I could calibrate) with a night on the big town. Stompin' at the Savoy. Could either of us still stomp? And what would it feel like to be in a minority with all those rhythmic, dancing coons? Well, at least old Benny would be white.

Just getting there was an adventure, even in Brünnhilde, our rebuilt-by-me-with-some-help pre-war Dodge. The great Black Way! The widest boulevard in Harlem. But where the hell do you park on 141st Street and Seventh? How far away would make the walk too dangerous for whities? Or for the exhausted to stagger back?

Once inside, of course, the crowd was mixed and friendly, but of course music, they say, hath special charms to soothe the savage. And savage they were, these darkies. Watching them go at it, an aristocracy of uptown taste, style, and grandeur, a garden of skin tones from almost white to African blue-black, strutting their stuff, flashing their finery, the cream of the crop and no doubt the cream of the crookèd, twirling and jiving, bucking and pivoting, the women flying in the air, caught by their partners…If I ever tried to pull that stuff with Dierdre, she'd shatter. Not that I could. So we sat out most of the dances except the slow ones, just taking in the battle of the bands.

The mammoth Savoy presented one continuous ritual, with bands playing from one bandstand while the next set up on the bandstand by its side. By this time, its clientele had spread to include rich whites, movie stars, visiting Europeans. But even though Benny Goodman played three times that night, I didn't see any caucasian royalty there, and we didn't really count.

Sitting out the dances, though, was a great way to spy upon my darling. If I sat to the side, and slightly behind her, I could watch the direction of her gaze, and measure its duration. This wasn't a stopwatch affair, and there was always the factor of dancers so spectacular that any woman, even in the most faithful of couples, would drop her jaw and hold her breath in applause.

Still, a sensitive like myself can know what's up, and I have to say that Deirdre passed the test with flying colors, except for almost falling asleep by ten. A bottle of coke took her to midnight, and back to Brünnhilde, a few blocks away.

Deirdre's being completely innocent of roving eye was something of a relief, but actually complicated my problem. If our storied romance was becoming buried under a blanket of fatigue and dirty diapers, if the fairyland princess was metamorphosing into a frog (well, not quite) and her prince into a baldpate — what then?

Madame de Stael noted that while the desire of the man is for the woman, the desire of the woman is for the desire of the man. She may or may not be right, but since she was putatively a woman, I'll give her the benefit of the doubt.

The reader can see in this analysis how dependent a successful marital relationship is on continual male desire. Or in any relationship. As my attachment clouded over, I sought a replacement to excite me. Cheating on my wife and young family was too predictable, too bourgeois, finally too boring, and would no doubt end me up in a similar draining situation if my mistress, too, grew older and fatter. I needed some object for my impatient affections to be ever stylish and shapely, ever new, renewing or renewable, ever tunable, understandable without my needing to be a PhD or a saint, some situation easily lubricated — human, soft and pliable, unencumbered by diapers, sleep, or snowsuits.

As I jiggled off an oil pan one summer morning, my hands spattered with still-warm oil — epiphany! I realized the solution, the long-term solution, was staring at me from the lift above. I would throw myself into something universally acclaimed, not societally condemned, something that would reflect well on me, and shower benefits on a Deirdre and offspring innocent of my cheating. I would stop being a grease-monkey whom the girls would be ashamed of in school. I would wear a suit snazzy enough to match my good, if balding, looks. I would lift myself, Hegelian-like, out of the working class into the stratospheric middle. I would become a used car salesman. How's that for adequately modest hubris?

I acknowledge that these days, as cars have become less mechanical, ever more brilliantly scientific, evolving each year, used cars have taken a reputational beating, besmirching those who would sell them as well. New, new, new. But what about less expensive than new? We (yes, now "we" — I am a successful car dealer) used car dealers would be the pastors of the postwar American soul. Upward mobility first required mobility, and those who most needed to rise were most in need of inexpensive vehicles. Let the plutocrats drive the luxury vehicles to which they are accustomed. But what about Mr. and Mrs. Joe Schmoe? Don't they need wheels too? Wheels they can afford? And there are more of them, both wheels and Schmoes.

Private Schmoe had his Jeeps in the army, jeeps and tanks and planes. Was he to come home victorious to his triumphant USA just to trudge around depositing shoe leather? And what about his new housing out in the Levittowns? How was he to get to work in the morning from a utopia beyond the bus lines? His car was his clothing, his shelter, his spiritual food, his unique tool in evolution. Do you realize that no previous animal has ever developed wheels as part of its anatomy? We in used car sales are the liberators of the *Untermensch*.

Solidarity forever.

I was hired away from Dolan's by Leo Bushey of Bushey Auto. He wanted a salesman who could talk technical with those kind of annoying customers, and one who could also switch hit from showroom to garage when a mechanic called in sick. I was the perfect choice, and he knew it. He upped my pay 150%. He must have had plans for me.

For orientation, he took me to Cody's Bar.

"You're an honest guy, right?" he began.

"Of course," I responded, insulted he should think otherwise.

"I was afraid of that."

And thus began a car-salesman tutorial which should become a book, and maybe I'll write it after this one. But in brief:

The first unit concerned lying. Axiom: we don't call it "lying". In fact, it's not "lying" per se. We call it SM, strategic misrepresentation.

SM certainly avoids falsehood as such, or any legally defined perjury. Its tools (if my notes are complete) are hyperbole and distortion, analogy (unwarranted, but poetic) and its close cousin, the disingenuous anecdote, cultivation of fear, and, at the very worst, delicate untruths or inadvertent misstatements. All these, relentlessly repeated in the course of a sales session, constitute an art-form to some extent related to the agit-prop of our former allies. While not actually engaged in warfare, let's say at least that these are our armamentarium of semantic weapons. All of which can be used honestly, candidly, sincerely, to help the customer for his own good. Sometimes we call the game The Acrobat and the Lump.

I say "not actually engaged in warfare", but one can easily intuit the metaphorical connection. My thoughts concerned the apparent war of salesmen vs. customers, and the subsequent bonding which seemed to ensue. Here's the way I figure it.

Over millenia, cave men fighting large toothed beasts must have grouped together to protect one another, and also to enjoy, en masse, the excitement of being both hunter and hunted. Like other intense experiences, these thrills were interpreted as sacred — and the bonding and altruism that came with them. All together in a supreme life-threatening, life-affirming effort! Outside of that kind of engagement, life seems vapid, trivial, tedious. Battle makes us more real. A need for warlike engagement is simply practical wisdom. And playing The Acrobat and the Lump is fun.

"Lump" may sound a little harsh, but it is not without reality as a descriptor, at least of the psychic state of those sitting in car salesman's office or sniffing inexpertly at the innards of a used car. And "lump" has quite a wide range of expression, from the simply porridge-like to the scheming clod hoping to get the better of his betters.

Granted that most used car seekers are sufferers in need, and about to sacrifice what must be a great deal of money for them to alleviate their stranded situation. But when they try to joke about it — the clichés they resort to — they are frightening. Nevertheless I understand that lump pain is real.

Real but trivial, debased, their dreams warped by a uniquely American combination of naiveté and cynicism, failure awaits them all. Why? Because they are all so stupid it makes you wonder about the inerrancy of Nature's laws. They're all cut from the same cloth, fascinatingly deformed, almost, but not quite, resembling human beings. And what makes them so frightening is that in them I can detect those skinny-armed boys and flowering girls of my high school days, now sunk into fat so pervasive that their eyes are barely visible, all of them having permanently disappeared into the worlds of their exploiters.

More frightening still is the evidence that, *de profundis*, they are still dreaming the old dreams, still exhibiting a queer, rosily sentimental faith in the world. Though their lives are sour and shriveled, they would proclaim life to be "sweet". The tragic trinity: delusion, then will, then woe, and its even more tragic packaging.

I was disappointed in my fellow man.

Nevertheless, I was determined to help them, to teach my victims — if necessary via further victimization. I became a used car salesman at Bushey's.

Leo Bushey was a smart man, smart enough to know he had a potential genius under his wing. He gave me a long leash. As long as I brought in the suckers and the sales, he was content. And only a few months into my new job, so was I. My monthly sales were greater than those of any two of the other salesmen combined. Three cheers and hubba hubba. One can't be squeamish about self-praise. I practiced my leechdom on the afflicted.

Of course the other salesmen set quite a low bar. Tom, a bulky Brobdingnag with a massive face, was a victim of detailism. Michael was an insectoid man of manifold ineptitudes. Joe was slightly nuts, but harmless, so harmless as to rarely make a sale. I could tell he wasn't long for the job. And Edgar was likely the dullest human being currently alive, with something neurally amiss. Idiotically cheerful. Again, an easy rival to beat. In such a gang, it was easy to stand out.

"*Honi soit qui mal y pense*" said one of the signs over my desk — which saying served a double function. First, it intimidated my customers and put them in their place. Though their chairs were on the same level as mine behind the desk, the sign created the feeling that mine sat on a slight platform, and theirs in a slight depression. Second, though they didn't know it, "Honi soit qui mal y pense" was a brutally honest warning and reprimand, placing the blame for any suspicions or acrimony about our transactions directly on them, and exculpating me, who never thought myself doing evil, but only doing good.

It wasn't hard for me to smile throughout our dealings. A smile of wisdom. A smile of understanding. A smile beatific for any deal well-concluded. Some people can look you straight in the eye and convey bottomless depths of insincerity. I, on the other hand, could shower my good will with the merest glance. It was all in my posture, my little routines, my polished gems of benevolence. As I looked at their broken hands and ugly faces I was overwhelmed by the desire to help.

Comforting the poor in spirit is not that hard. It just takes a little talent with spiritual liniment. Needless to say, Tom, Michael, Joe and Edgar were unfamiliar with the practice. I doubt they were devout Catholics. *Kyrie eleison, Christe eleison, Kyrie eleison* – denied to them. I wasn't an altar boy all those years for nothing.

Occasionally I had to be mean, to jar my client-patients out of their slumbers. "Look at me when I talk to you," always got their attention and respect. I was sometimes compelled to scold, even to insult. "What do you mean, Mr. Garritano, laughing like that?" But overall, the gestalt was bracing, and my statistics were good. Great. My customers learned the lessons I set out to teach.

Although things would soon change drastically, had someone set out my biography at this point in my life, this is what they might have written (and please do not mistake this me for myself. Everyone lives life behind a wall of misunderstanding):

(I set down the summary "this" in the form of Hegelian dialectic, a core component of the The Transcendental Brotherhood of the Great H: Hyde, Houdini, Hitler, Heidegger, Heisenberg, Hegel, Hrothgar, Hoagy Carmichael, Heaven and Hell. The Great H: two firm pillars connected, communicating as one through the corpus callosum, standing stably on its own two feet unlike pathetic Fs and Ps, utterly non-capricious, like Os and Ds. Thesis — antithesis, implying an even greater synthesis, and auguring ceaseless *Aufhebung*, of which, more later).

Beginning with the WHITE-HAT PILLAR, of Charles Martin Hyde one would likely say:

— Without having a Christ complex, he was a religious man, his life a religious quest. Once an altar boy, he was forever tainted with good. His goal was to clean out the Augean stables of his age.

— He was, in his way, a genius, someone from whom mankind had something to learn, something it did not know before.

— He was a Man of Ideas, propelled by fact, logic and critical thinking. As such, he did not belong to the present age, but to some future age of more advanced development.

— He continually examined the values by which he lived, and for all his uniqueness, always made sincere attempts to be humble. And sometimes he did feel humbled, weary, a sub-vocalizer, as he said, "in the presence of the Great Mystery."

— (For those of you of the semi-Jungian persuasion) His Myers-Briggs category was ENFJ — extroverted, intuitive, feeling, judging without being judgmental — the archetype of the beloved Teacher.

— He loved much. He loved humanity. His heart was good, too good, gentle as the moon, and just as vulnerable. He judged sarcasm to be the language of the Devil, and generally renounced it.

— Yes, he did well for himself and his family, yet he did well by doing good, helping others learn by making their own mistakes and correctly blaming themselves.

— His work was his play, and his play was teaching the essence of the world.

— Finally (and this might have served as his epitaph), he was a citizen of ages yet to come.

Onward through the crossbar of "at the same time" or "but" to the BLACK-HAT PILLAR:

— He would never be rid of himself, a mean son-of-a-bitch. But his meanness was scrupulous meanness, always surgically directed at appropriate targets. His was a chilliness of character essential to his talent for ruling.

— He was an athlete of amorality, capable of being holy and evil at the same time.

— How did he get so smart? By being universally suspicious. By thoroughly embracing the Enlightenment Project of rational analysis, a privilege of strong individuals. He always required accurate information and was never influenced by the brutal, harebrained propaganda generated for the multitude. He valued all the empirical underpinnings of the world – Boyle's law, Newtonian physics, classic doctrines of evolution and genetic inheritance, the automobile, gravity, the Invisible Hand…

— He was therefore a creature of his own destiny, soulless, hard, finally free from convention and the twin millstones of love and duty.

— And yes he did have a proclivity for self-enhancement and accumulation.

When he let himself think about it, he felt like a shit – a real, first class, select, grade A, certifiable, not-approved-by-Good-Housekeeping shit.

Fair and balanced, wouldn't you say? A few more words

on the Good side than on the Bad, but qualities are often independent of quantities. *Apologia pro vita mea.*

Reading over the lists, at that point in my world-line I didn't know exactly where the road would take me, but I did know that there would likely be a higher synthesis, an *Aufhebung*, an awakening. There was always a something offering itself, an urge, a movement directed toward something entirely different, a something that sought a very different relationship with the something which was then me.

And for me, that something was Meshugeneh Moses , MM, "Moish".

6. MOISH

The sign was huge, a welded sculpture of auto parts almost fifty feet high. I paced off its shadow in the late afternoon when my own was equal to my height. It seemed to have four sections. Revolving on an axial steel pole, the lower section was some kind of geometric construction, which I attempted to capture with the following sketch:

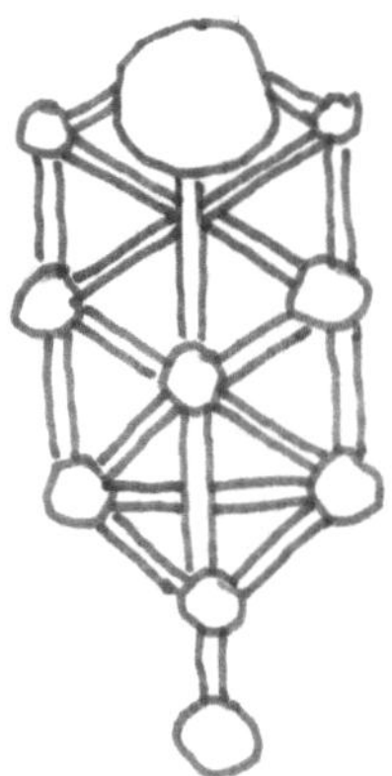

The circles shown were fashioned from one floodlight, and nine freestanding headlamps scavenged, I imagine, from twenties or early thirties models, the kind that stood on top of front fenders, not recessed within them. The paths connecting them were made from old driveshafts and muffler pipes, painted orange. The whole array stood about ten feet high.

Rising above the floodlight on top was a twenty-foot humanoid figure, which I soon learned was a huge sculpture of the owner of the new car lot, himself, while human no doubt, did give off a humanoid impression. The likeness, it turned out, was decent, but through the framing of his body, one could easily see a larger reproduction of the geometric sculpture below, with variegated hubcaps anchoring his head, ears and shoulders, one at his heart, one at each knee, one at the groin, and one hubcap between his legs, sitting right atop the upper headlamp, and looking comically like a turd inadvertently dropped.

The figure's right arm was raised above his head, and was somehow supporting a 1943 Hudson which, it turned out, was the first car the owner ever sold. Another ten feet stacked precariously on. I am not enough of an engineer to predict its stability, or enough of artist to depict the whole. But you can well imagine how astonishing the affair was for workaday Paterson. How the skeletal structure could support a '43 Hudson off center was beyond me unless it was merely the external body, sans guts. The owner later asserted it was not, it was the whole car, repurchased from its owner for its current exalted position. But who would dare climb up there to check?

Atop the whole, making up the fifty feet, and creating the shape of a mushroom cloud, was the neoned name of the new emporium —

MESHUGENEH MOISHE'S
Great Deals on Wheels!
Marvellously Stupid Prices!!!

A trip to the library for a dictionary (I suspected it was Yiddish) yielded up the following: "Meshugeneh: Crazy, nuts, wildly extravagant." It certainly fit the sculpture.

But the strangest thing of all is that it appeared overnight. I walked or drove past that lot on Grand Street several times a week, and could swear that the day before, it was just the big, old empty lot we kids use to play king of the rock in when I was growing up. Different garbage perhaps, but as empty as lots get in Paterson.

Helicoptered in in modules and constructed overnight? And the paving, and the fifty cars, and the medium-sized showroom?

The sign stood over Paterson like the Eiffel Tower over Paris, built for eternity. One could only gaze at it in wonder. Wonder and perhaps incipient horror. I thought of Poe's "City in the Sea"

From a proud tower in the town
Death looks gigantically down.

I went back the next day to check my sanity. Hanging at eye level was an incongruously hand-lettered sign:

HELP WANTED. THIS MEANS YOU.
CLOSED SATURDAYS.

It was Saturday.

Did the sign mean he was open on Sundays? Why not? Not much else going on, and shopping for a used family car was as amusing as anything else going on Sundays in Paterson. It was probably a brilliant sales scheme. Not being a church-goer, I returned the next morning at ten, and stepped into a brilliantly lighted showroom which, like the sign/sculpture outside it, had appeared, I swear, overnight.

"Vhat took you so long? Ve've been open since six."

The speaker was a little man, stumping along toward me, very little, actually, more like a dwarf, but very quick — like a monkey.

"You missed de best part of de morning, vhen de light begins to light, and all de Muse girls go dencing by. At six, de voild is megic, and you are sleeping? Sit down, ve'll talk. End I do not accept an insenity defense."

He plopped down in a huge chair behind an ornately carved desk completely out of step with the post-war modern of the showroom.

He stared at me through an awkwardly long silence,

expecting me to start. I had no idea what to say, though it seemed up to me.

"How come you aren't open on Saturdays, like everyone else?"

"So who says I'm like everyone else? You hoid of de sabbath? Shabot? Sabados? De day of rest. You got to rest sometime. Saturn's day. You know from Saturn?"

"It's a big planet."

"Planet, feh! Saturn is a god. Fertilidy, velth, liberation. You vant some liberation?"

"No…er, well, maybe."

He was the worst dance partner ever.

"Maybe, huh? From vhat? Liberation from vhat?"

I needed to pull out of this conversation.

"Wait a minute. You were the one who said you needed help. The sign outside — on the sign, the big sign, the sculpture, or whatever it is."

"You vant to know vhat is it?"

"Well, yeah, sure."

"Vhat it is, you kent understend. Too mysterious. But I'll give you a hint. It's me. Dats me up dere, holding de foist car I ever sold. End det's my name, Moish, in case you couldn't figure it out. End det's my motto — deals on wheels, stoopid prices."

"I understood all that. But the stuff holding it all up, the erector set thing on the bottom…"

"Erector set — det's funny. I never hoid det before. In hunderts of years."

"So what do you call it?"

"Vhat do I call it? I call it vhat it's called!"

"Which is?"

(I thought I had him on the run.)

"Det's for me to know, and you to find out. Go study. But I'll give you a hint. It begins vit a S."

"And all those car headlamps?"

"Dey light up."

"I assumed so."

"And ven all ten are lit de same time, de foist person who comes in to say so, gets a free car."

"What? How can you make any money?"

"Dey don't all ten light up at de same time a lot. But it keeps people looking, vatching. Makes for good stories in de pehpers."

This is my memory of my first meeting with Moish. I didn't know whether to be charmed and amused or to run like hell. But in the interest of learning some quirky tricks for my own imagined car lot, and after consultation with Deirdre (she consulting her Tarot cards), I decided to accept his offer to sign on as a salesman at twice my then-salary with Dolan.

The free car was always of course the worst on the lot, likewise in the "buy-an-accessory (like an MM license plate frame or a side view mirror, or a steering wheel cover) and-get-a-free-car-to-go-with-it" sales, the accessories cost the would-have-been price of the car, and the Days of Awesome

Insanity featured only an entire staff dressed as clowns, all tempted with bonuses for the most outrageous behavior.

In other words, Meshugeneh Moish was not as meshugeneh as he pretended to be, but a phenomenally original businessman, who quickly drew all of Paterson's warm attention to his obviously fraudulent, but truly whacky style.

And, alone among the other salesmen, I kept getting unexplained bonuses.

I should introduce the crew, not because they themselves were crucial in my story, but because they were my inadvertent mentors in car salesmanship. Mentor, of course, would have cringed at the comparison.

They were Ed, Bud and Al, collectively and comparatively all pathetic in sales volume compared to me.

Ed Toffelmeier was a big guy, half a foot taller than I, dull of face, but at the right moments he could look like Clark Kent when he takes off his glasses. His thick, greasy hair gave me a hint of what he must have been like in high school (before my time) — one of those would-be criminal types forever being suspended or sent to the principal, someone you'd expect to drop out of school to go work on his uncle's garbage truck. But he had matured into a merely large person, always concerned with how to dispose of his hands or feet, but mildly avuncular, even if he was cursed with evil breath. Gullibility was his greatest blessing. As a salesman, a generous B-.

Clarence "Bud" Malone was a man miserable in body, mind, and spirit. He seemed to have overly-washed himself, perhaps with lye soap, as if he had understood some large and terrible truth. On his face, a deadpan sullenness, or, as the Russians say "On him there is no face", an idiom describing utter dejection. He did not look at, but only sideways-glanced at things and people, with a kind of sigh in that glance, followed by a nasally hissing inbreath. He was like some high priest of futilitarianism — none of his projects, great or small, ever worked out. His ensuing take on human existence was that of inevitability, unrealizability, and irrevocability. You can imagine his sales grade: C-. In God's name, I don't know why Moishe kept him on. Perhaps out of pity. Merciful Moish.

Big Al Toricino was far shorter than I, but big he was — I'd say about 350 pounds. I never asked. He actually resembled a blowfish. A very nice guy, but I don't think his brain was working too well. "I got mercury poisoning," he used to explain, "I suffer from stupid." His was a pleasant, stolid sort of idiocy, and he never seemed worried about anything. I gather he didn't know enough to be worried. And he meant so well. But when one has a Big Al sort of heart, it is silly being too resolute about anything. He was another pitiable specimen, but unlike Bud, a tad ridiculous. The chartreuse suede shoes didn't help. With his comical fat-man's peppiness, was actually a decent salesman. I'd give him a B+

But finally, what a collection of inept clowns! No wonder I was Moish's favorite. Nevertheless, from that teaching

faculty I learned the basic style of successful salesmanship
— by contrast. Armed with Moish's instruction concerning
strategic misrepresentation, and with the constant examples
of Ed, Bud, and Big Al playing out before my eyes, I became
— I'm not ashamed to say — one of the big, if anony-
mous, names in used cars sales. It was Meshugeneh Moish
who racked up the numbers, but I was the chief racker, the
eminence grise, the man behind the madman — and Moish
knew it. I was a smart recruitment for him, and perhaps
his retaining the others was his specific pedagogical method
concerning ways not to be, his array of Thou-Shalt-Nots. I
knew he had plans for me, but what they were I could barely
imagine.

Some of the credit for my meteoric rise must go, too, to
the car-hungry citizens of Paterson, New Jersey. I don't know
what the mean IQ is in my home town, but I imagine it must
be far below that of, say, New York City, not 20 miles to the
east. P. T. Barnum, Deirdre's extra-curricular instructor as she
grew up in Bridgeport, famously said, "There's a sucker born
every minute," though recent scholarship claims this is apoc-
ryphal. I, however, would add an intensifier: In Paterson, New
Jersey, there must be a sucker born at least every ten seconds.

You could see it on their faces — anxious naiveté, exuding
a need to be gulled. They usually arrived in the showroom
with complex, but manipulative, confusion written all over
them. O, Grantor of Cars, have mercy and shower benefi-
cence upon us. Pretty please.

When I smile, and address them gently and patiently they instinctively trust me. Their instincts are wrong. They either arrive alone, fat, unclean-looking men, deeply immersed in problems of physical and mental hygiene, hideous and terrible; or they arrive in couples, fat women rolling or waddling in, sometimes in the company of brisk, lively, jesting fat men, (Big Al was good with these fat, amorous turtles, weighed down by the *merde* of their existence.) Or worst of all, young males, groping, anxious to succeed, all steamed up with resentment against things they have no notion of. Cruisin' for a brusin', they are.

I obviously can't deliver their fantasies, their moronic, lovely dreams which always refuse to come true. Their thinking has disappeared into their thinking, their volition into what it is they want, their belief dissolving into what they believe. Nevertheless I labor in my role as teacher, and I engage in the Great Game.

Moish's strategies were original, brilliant, and inspiring — at least to me. The monthly Sunday brunches appealed to us all, even if he used these mandatory celebrations to preach his mysterious life strategies. His "lessons", he called them. Our attendance was payment for the sumptuous sandwiches he provided.

Some talks flirted with the pedestrian, the one on his Philosophy of Clothes, for instance. But always they hinted at something deeper. Titled "I Kesh Clothes!" it developed the intimate connections between clothing and cash. Clothes making and unmaking the impression of the man, clothes defining kless structure, mesters and slaves, clothes creating the material conteners that hid the core of being. "And vhat is beeing? Det's for you to find out." (His most oft-repeated expression.) But clothes, he warned, "in de voild of appearances," are often seen as more important than the truth they cover.

How were we to apply this wisdom? We were all to wear clown suits every Friday. He would supply them according to his understanding of the nature of our souls. We could take them with us if we decided to move on. "Just a liddle experiment. Ve goink to see how de seles voik out."

I actually refused at first. I thought it beneath my dignity. "You know vhat's dignified?" he asked me, with his most intense gaze. "Etoinity. Dat's vhat's dignified. And vhat are you compared?" I took his point (and wanted to keep my job), and asked if I could use some of *his* clothes as my clown costume. He wasn't insulted. "Vhat good taste you hef, bubeleh." So on Fridays, I got to dress up as Mishugeneh Moish, in the great tradition of the Feast of Fools, with the last being first. "Every velley shell be exaltid. Det's you," the Boss said.

"*Deposuit potentes*," I countered, hoping to gain some advantage from my Jesuit ed.

"Det's rite," he said, "But who is Mr. Potentes?" he asked with some Groucho twitching of his eyebrows." And he pointed half up in the air, and half to indicate he'd made a point. Which I didn't quite get at the time.

Many of his sermons were about "Gott". I didn't much mind them. In my altar boy days, I had always liked the sermons best since I didn't have to do anything during them. Al Toricino and Bud Malone were probably Catholics, and Ed Toffelmeier, could have been anything, but even Lutherans have sermons, don't they? We all worked Sunday mornings, so Moishe's brunches were our stand-in church.

Ever a goody-two-shoes academically, I usually took notes, half to impress the Boss, and half because I thought the ideas might be useable in the future. Here is my best reconstruction of an early homily to help us better understand our salesmen tasks.

Vhat are you kvetching? Because you don't hev de best, de most lovely customers? You vant a poifect woild vid your clients? (We nod our heads.) Gott also vants a poifect voild. But how to get one? Gott says to himself, "I vould like to make a perfect world." So vhat does He do? He makes men and vimmen and he looks on them squvinting his eyes and says, "Hmmm," end he paces around, tinking, tinking, end all de liddle humans jump up and down hocking a chinek, yelling "Vhen do we start, vhen do we start?"

So Gott is sitting on his stoop, end vatching how is everybody behaving. End dets vhen all de tsouris begins, everyting, all de tings dey yell about in books end newspapers, vawrs, crime, violence, adultery, end all de tings you complain about here, even in Moishe's used car heaven. Gott tinks to himself how he ken make a poifect voild. Hmmmm. Dere's a mistake here, it von't never voik! He picks up a liddle human being, some big macher's son, end trows him in de pot. Den he sees a liddle goil, cute, a sheyna meydela, but she's a bed liddle goil, so into de pot with her! Dis udder vun is terrible – same ting – into de pot vit it! Dis one is ok, dis one is pretty nice, a gud Samaritan or someting, end over dere, a Knaz Myshkin poisen, valking around in de field carefully not to step on voims. Nice. Very nice.

But.

Dere's always a "but", because a poifect voild he vants to make, and no one is poifect. But Gott is trying anyway. He figures dis is not de finished copy, so into de pot vit de gud Samaritan, into de pot with Knaz Myshkin, into de pot vit de whole everybody! Yes! Now Gott is a cook, and he vants tings glatt kosher. In de pot he's making a stew, and from det stew is going to make a nice broth, end out of det broth he's going to make vun boiled-down liddle drop of poifect essence, end det's vhat he's going to start his real-hearts-desire voild with, det drop from de broth of de stew in the pot.

He sat down, and began eating his pastrami sandwich. We waited for him to clear his mouth and continue. He just kept biting away and chewing, thirty chews for each bite — his prescription for good health. After a couple of minutes, Ed, slow but steady, spoke for us all:

"So what's the end of the story?"

"I told you vhat is de end of de story. Det's de end of de story, vhat I told."

"But I don't get it," Big Al admitted.

"Det's your problem," Moish said, "Cless dismissed." And, chomping away, he gestured us to return to the show-room, the lot.

7. MY WOMEN

Beauty has always been my undoing, whether the siren-song of a well-tuned Model A, or the siren-rise of Annabel's chest as she breathed Josquin's *Ave Maria* from under her choir gown. It is no grammatical accident that we call our cars "she".

As my bank account increased, my sense of mission intensified, and as my still-mostly-lovely once-sylph of a wife became sylph no more, it was only natural for my eyes to begin to wander, and for the rest of me below the belt occasionally to follow. I'm sure at least my male confessors will grant me this.

Add to the temperature change in my attraction to Deirdre the six continuous years of dirty diapers, followed by six more of snowsuit ons and offs, plus six more of what-do-I-know-about-small-girls, and you have a formula encouraging little fissures in fidelity.

But even all together, they didn't weigh as much in the infidelity equation as one thing which I have hinted at, but which lately had grown into a continuous irritation: Deirdre's infatuation with the fatuous stupidity of astrology.

Though it sounds more like Yogi Berra, "Prediction is very difficult, especially if it's about the future" is a quote attributed to Niels Bohr. And *he* was a Nobel Prize winner. But for Deirdre it was alarmingly simple. All one had to do was to cast a chart (she was quick at this) for the person asking advice (or open to hearing it) for the time and place of the intended activity, and then to see what planets would be transiting what astrological houses in those hours, and what angles they would be making one with another.

Which superstitions threw me into regular tizzies. They were blots on the human brain, some morbid fealty to darkness rather than the light of modern science.

"You don't believe in astrology," she would say, "because you're a Scorpio and Scorpios are skeptical."

That recursive gambit in pillow-talk concerning the validity of astrology, summarizes the problem — intensely and in depth.

To it she would add that Scorpios always need to have clear knowledge. "But on the other hand, Charlie, Scorpios are potentially the greatest mystics with unsurpassed creative power. They are natural storytellers, interested in all human experience just like you. I predict one day you'll write a great book. You really should look into these things." This flattery also explains why I would never leave her.

Nevertheless, every time I saw her pouring over the daily astrological inanities in the *Star-Ledger*, or heard her warning the children about this being a bad day for this or for that, I had to tamp down my rage. Her world just didn't match up to the world-world. She flits around in a pre-Copernican geocentric universe, circa 1507. She is a Pisces — she likes shiny things.

It began fairly innocently with her studying Tarot cards. Even a poker player like me can appreciate the fascinating designs and the symbolism they wield. Then, when it came out to such applause in 1950, she got hold of the English translation of the *I Ching*. Again, its charm is evident, its place in Chinese culture and history central. But when she asked me to bring her yarrow stalks from my next trip to Chinatown, and when meanwhile she began consulting kitchen skewers for answers to important family questions, channeling answers from the Zhou dynasty and acting upon them, my patience was sorely tested.

But her predictive astrology took the cake away, and did actually dislodge much sweetness from our home life, now infested by the stars.

Needless to say, the drop in romance temperature put her in a vulnerable condition, for in spite of my baldness, my otherwise good looks continued to send women into a frenzy, Betties and Veronicas both, good girls and bad, Vassar girls from Westchester, barmaids with jawsfull of gum — it seemed as if between the months of April and July, and then again in Septembers and Octobers bevies of frantic women were rushing into the used car lot hoping to impregnate themselves upon me. I remember a year or two ago, when Chatty Cathys first came out, and during a shopping tour with Deirdre and the girls, I pulled the ring on a demo doll's back to see what the fuss was all about. "I love you," she squeaked, and then on the next pull, "Take me to bed with you." I high-tailed out of there pretty fast. You can believe me or not, but every one of these propositions, and not just Chatty Cathy's, I turned down. It offended my sense of manhood not to do the asking.

The dynamic was instructive. Because my occasional lust-and-loneliness targets seemed to freeze up when leered at, I learned the value of cool. As a married father of three, I couldn't exactly do the zoot suit thing, especially with the duck's ass topping, but that didn't keep me from eyeing the girls who hung around on corners, and passing them closely by on my walk home, suave and detached enough to turn their pretty little heads.

But under the right (wrong) circumstances, cool can get hot pretty quickly. My first extramarital adventure occurred on a Saturday morning at the public library downtown. Moish exhorted us to use our Sabbaths to study — he often answered "Go study!" to questions — but with a very partic-ular exception: If we were going to study on Saturday days off in the Paterson Public Library, we should avoid books that had the library's name stamped on the top, bottom, or side edges of the pages. Or expect punishment if we didn't.

His answer to "Why is that?" was, "Go study!" It seemed too weird a prohibition not to. None of the librarians knew, so I figured it was either some insane Moishism, or related to the enigmatic religious principles he seemed to emanate.

But *all* the books on Judaism, or Judaica, had PPL stamped along the bottom. What to do? I was examining book after book, checking only the bottoms, when I noticed a young woman watching me suspiciously. I examined her with my excellent peripheral vision, looking and looking away at the same time. She was wearing black stockings under a very quiet blue dress, but I assure you I was so disturbed I almost dropped the heavy book I was holding. Her dark beauty was maddening.

When she noticed I had noticed her noticing me, she asked, non-aggressively, "Why are you looking at the bottoms of all those books?"

She must have been watching me for a while, for at least three examinations worth to justify an "all those" descriptor. Did she find me so attractive?

Our hearts met, I thought, in our eyes.

"My boss ordered me not to open books with print along the page edges."

"Anytime?"

"No. Just on Saturdays. Weird, huh?" (I had her talking, engaged in conversation without even trying.)

"Ah. The *melakhot.*"

"The what?"

"*Melakhot*. The 39 prohibited activities."

She turned to go. I reached out and touched her shoulder before she turned out of the aisle. She grabbed my hand, spun round, examined the guilty fingers, then looked me in the eye.

"You can tell a nonkosher bird by its talons."

She spun back around, and disappeared into the stacks. I knew better than to pursue. Thus, my first love encounter with a Jewish woman.

Sunday morning, no customers in the showroom, I requested a private tutorial from Moish on Saturday library book prohibitions. Because he realized I was the only one of his boys that might consider a Saturday library visit, he invited me into his showroom office for a consult.

Gott, he reminded me, worked for six days, and then rested. I went along for the sake of argument. He rested from his creative work (*melakhot*). Since we, and particularly bald, handsome me, were created in the image of Gott, we, too, had to rest from creative work on our mandatory rest days. Over the centuries, respected Rabbis had identified 39 activities that involved prohibited creative work — work exercising power over one's environment. Two of them were writing and erasing.

I'm not sure anyone but editors would agree with the latter, but there are probably a lot of Jewish editors.

"So?" I asked him. I hadn't been writing or erasing, just wanting to look in some books to try to figure him out.

"You are not kepable to figure me out. Unlike viceh voisa."

I held my hands palm up in surrender.

"De qvestion is wedder opening such a book vit writing on de edges is ectually erasing, and wedder closing it again is ectually writing "PEHTESIN PUBLIC LIBRERRY". So vhat do you tink?"

I couldn't tell him I thought the whole question was silly.

"You tink de hole qvestion is silly."

"…."

"Okeh, det's vhat *you* tink. Geh vek, and don't sin no more."

This man was inscrutable. More than inscrutable.

OK, extracurricular women — that's what you've all been waiting for.

For readers who like to have everything explained precisely…the truth is, I don't have much to say or confess. My primary adulterous affair was with my left hand, an exercise in onanism which may be damaging to the soul, but which has saved many men (and women perhaps?) from aspiring to some greater silliness, and endangering their matrimonial endeavors.

One actual adultery was so memorable that it put the kibosh on many subsequent ones. I was "away on a business trip", "car shopping out of state for Moish". I-forget-her-name and I were lying side by side in the moonlight on the shore of a small pond behind her country home. Nuzzles led to snuggles, and some preliminary unbuttoning. And then, "I can't tonight, Charlie."

"Why? Why not?" I urged, reaching around for her bra strap.

"Because I've got the farts. Bad. Too uncomfortable."

A rather large crack in the Grecian urn. What could I do but laugh, and give up? But thereafter, whenever I even thought of reaching for a bra strap, I could — Rimbaud synaesthia, Proustian recall — smell fart. And a fart imagined can be even worse, at least in its implications, than a real live fart encountered. Imagination — an effective anti-aphrodisiac, easily packaged, though anti-aphrodisiacs are a hard sell these days.

The diaper-exhaustion cooling of our original passion had just begun to give way to a slight warming trend when once again, Deirdre became strangely removed, distracted, "too tired", "not-tonight-dear-I-have-a-headache"-y. My first thought was that now that the kids were all toddling, she imagined it was time for her to take a lover. But I couldn't sustain that suspicion. Nothing else checked. I steamed open any hand-written envelopes that, from the handwriting, might have come from male admirers (for she was still gorgeous, in a more earthy way). Nothing learned except how to reseal more professionally. I made sure I was the one to answer the phone if we were both at home. She thought I was just being considerate. Some days, instead of taking lunch hour, I scurried home for an unexpected surprise visit. Again, I'm sure she interpreted it in a positive way. But again — nothing.

So to plot a survival scheme for a 40% marriage, I made a list of all the qualities I'd look for in a love-replacement that would not replace, but only supplement. When I'd finished with the obvious physiognomical categories, and begun on the more spiritual ones, I thought to myself, "Isn't this just a little ridiculous, Charlie? Sitting down with your lined note-book like an accountant, deciding what to fall in love with? Why not just love? Fall unexpectedly in love. You see some-one and in that instant, you give up your rows and columns, and can't help yourself." So I settled for that. Even tore out the pages I was working on in case Deirdre should happen to come across them — if *she* were snooping.

It did cross my mind that perhaps D had another kind of secret she was pondering in her heart. I had just read a new poem of Sylvia Plath's about a miscarriage she'd suffered, the inconspicuous absence, unreadable by others, the fetus's cry fading "like the cry of a gnat." Perhaps there had been a gnat between Deirdre and me, but I didn't have the heart to ask.

So — of extracurricular women, not much to tell. But of curricular women — there were more and more coming into play. Together, they made up The Sisters Hyde.

I present them this way because rather than insisting on their own individuality, they were — from earliest — one for all and all for one. A slight to one was resented and punished by three. They were living examples of The New Soviet Man, except they were little girls.

They didn't have to insist on their individuality because they were all so different, as if they had been made in different factories, using different designers and engineers. Cooie, Looie, and Dooie — Carolyn, Louisa, and Dorothy — all variations on the physical theme of Deirdre, all apples of my eye, and they all drove me nuts. They never want money, they never wanted money, they didn't understand why I wanted to make money, or so much money.

I had a plan to name them Eenie, Meenie, Miney, and Moe – but Moe never came along — or maybe he did and gnatted out of here fast. You know, the world might be a lot better without names, clearer, purer, more unlimited, less loving. Also less hating.

But they liked their names, their nicknames, and enjoyed coming on collectively as "the Oooies" (conjugation: *Ooowie, ooo*wie, ooo*wie*). Once one said or wanted anything, they would chant it together so that the most innocent observation or demand wound up arriving on the triple tines of pitchforks. The Triplets of War and Revolution. The Andrews Sisters had nothing on them.

I thought first to categorize them according to the wisdom of a nursery rhyme. Perhaps you recall

Monday's child is fair of face,
Tuesday's child is full of grace,
Wednesday's child is full of woe,
Thursday's child has far to go,
Friday's child is loving and giving,
Saturday's child must work for a living,
But the child that's born on the Sabbath day,
Is fair and wise and good and gay.

Deirdre was popping them out annually, and their birthdays were all clustered around Valentine's Day — February 12th, 14th, and 15th. Cooie was certainly fair of face, but having "far to go" was not a very encouraging prediction. Looie, according to the wise Mama Goose, would have to work for a living, but so do we all, so do we all. Dooie, however, hit the jackpot, and in fact was fair and wise and good and gay. One out of three, however, did not make the Goose's an attractive interpretive system. I came to realize that they had fallen like roulette balls into a three-compartment wheel contrived in the classic body, mind, and spirit compartments. Body, Mind, and Spirit (in that order) was much more predictive. Increasingly dematerialized.

They seemed to be three monads, but they could and would come together like a major or minor triad, in various inversions, their personhoods still distinct, yet possessing a powerful common effect. By the time they were eight, nine, and ten, they had pledged themselves to one another, exchanged rings, pricked their forefingers with a thorn and licked each other's blood. But since, like Muses and Norns, they helped shape my destiny, I shall try to describe them singly.

Cooie, my firstborn. I suppose all babies are born ugly. I mean if you saw an adult walking around with the body and face of a newborn, you'd run for the first public toilet to throw up, right? And I suppose, too, that all first time fathers are secretly shocked when their spawn is held up for them to admire. Not a tactful thing to say out loud, but I know what they all think as they look at their exhausted wives: "What monster with my name have you delivered up into the world? Why did I ever marry you?" Why are first time fathers famously afraid to touch the womb's issue? QED.

When they did shame me into holding her I was struck by how like a piece of meat she was. Nine or so pounds of veal, maybe. Her cry gave me the shivers, like nails on a blackboard. She smelled like, I don't know, words fail me, icky — and it would get worse until she learned to better control her excretions. What could any male love about these things? And think of the expenses coming up, the sleepless nights, the doctor bills, the extra alcohol to be consumed just to forget it all for a moment. Really, there's not much initially going for being a dad.

But in spite of the initial reality, I dutifully imagined her growing up to become an Irish beauty like her mom — and immediately began worrying about the pimply faced adolescents intent on seducing little girls. I'd defend that bridge when I came to it. But my hackles were already up.

I have to admit that things soon got better. According to Dr. Williams, Cooie was a healthy child, quick to crawl, then toddle, then walk, then run. Her language learning was the marvel all parents experience. How did she figure out grammatical complexity? Where did she pick up that word? By the time Looie came along a year later, and Dooie, two, we had the affective routine down, and as long as Deirdre did most of the work, we could sail along as good-looking young parents, three times blessed, effectively stowed away from military service.

Parents, I warn you — never let a sensitive young girl read Wittgenstein. I came home for dinner one night when she was in eighth grade to find Cooie "off" as we used to say. Depressed or something. When I asked what was bothering her, she burst out crying, sobbing, in fact. Aha! It was no doubt some blind, passionate attachment to some older cad who had taken advantage of her naive credulity. Now was the time to set her straight on the subject of birds, bees, and men.

But no. What was she so upset about? A question Wittgenstein once posed to his students (Oh, come on! What is this really about?) (No, really, dad...): So you tie a string around the earth at the equator — very tightly, so you can't even slip your pinky under it. Don't worry about the mountains or the oceans (OK, I won't worry) Now you snip it apart, and add one yard more of string. This much. (OK) And smooth out all the slack so the circle stands out equally all around the earth. (My patience is waning with this shaggy dog story. There'd better be a good punchline.) How high off the earth do you think the string is standing?

"That's it? That's what you're upset about?"

"How high?"

"What are you so upset about?"

"How high?"

"I don't know. Who knows? Probably you couldn't tell. Like adding a bucket of water to the ocean."

"Almost six inches!" she proclaimed, and began to cry again. "The answer would be the same for the earth, the sun, or the moon." And her wailing increased. "Or a goddamned tennis ball. (She didn't usually swear. That's how upset she was.)

If ever a father didn't understand child-rearing, this was it. All I could do was to comfort her, and to tell her that everything would be all right.

But of course, the first thing I did after she had retired, was to attempt to resurrect my good old high school geometry and algebra, $C = 2\pi r$, that sort of thing. It was easy enough — add to C, and solve for the new r — and by god, she and that Austrian pansy were right. 5.73 inches, to be exact, totally independent of the initial circumference.

Something was wrong with the relationship between human intuition and reality. Of course, we knew that already, but not in so stark a demonstration. I had to admit it might be worth getting upset about, especially if I were a fourteen year old girl, secretly in love with a sex-driven cad. Anyway I relate this incident as a key to understanding a Cooie assaulted by mathematics. How innocent she had appeared in the sexless light of childhood.

Looie, the Saturday's child that would have to work for a living. Well, maybe that wasn't so far off, or even deplorable, if, as later, I took it to understand her devotion to "the working class". Little Louise, Lulu the Lunatic, began reading and spouting Marx before she was even a teen. She held a study group for her teenybopper friends, which didn't last long. Their motto? *"The devaluation of the human world increases in direct relation to the increase in value of the world of things.* Economic And Philosophical Manuscripts Of 1844."

Are those words that ever should cross a little girl's lips?

We should have predicted it. As a babe, she used to seize poor Deirdre by the nipple with her sharp little teeth, and sometimes draw blood. We put her early on the bottle.

A silent, moody child, meditative, disgruntled, an early reader, easily hurt, and often scorned by her peers, much too sensitive to withstand the ridiculous buffoonery and brutality, the acquisitive carelessness of post-war America, she would ramble, moping, under the dripping trees on our block, her hands buried in the pockets of her green vinyl raincoat, she would brood on the horror of life, and, unlike her older sister, come back to report her analyses to her stodgy parents, complete with childish schemes for a communist utopia. Her five-year old — but memorable — analysis of observable power structures: "They are all stupids!" She had quite a future ahead of her if Sen. McCarthy didn't take her down first.

Adolescent daydreaming was not for her. No man on a white horse galloped through the pages of a locked, personal diary in a dark corner of her dresser. Or if it existed, I never found it. She claimed to document all her thoughts in a publicly available set of notebooks.

The domestic searchlight of her all-engulfing skepticism centered on her mother's mystical fog. Far beyond any opiate-of-the-masses critique, she carefully clipped each day's astrological forecast from the Paterson Evening News, and paired them with the next day's reports of events, local, national, and international. Her dinner talk would include a daily report of "zero correspondence", which must have saddened Deirdre, not as having disproved anything, but because of the rigidness of her daughter's mind.

But her primary target was of course me, Mister Bourgeois, a spider without a conscience, smiling my smiles, cheating my impoverished customers, selling them a fraudulent dream of Freedom in a carcerative America, a Babbit on the warpath, unaware that given capitalism, everything is going to fall apart, all structures based on greed and so-called morality were going to rot away, that we all would soon get cankers on our hearts, crustaceans would cling to our brains, and our lungs will collapse and crumble. How could I be so stupid as not to see this? The symptoms were staring me in the face.

"Even Moishe?" I asked, hoping to lighten the discourse.

"A clown."

As the clown would say, "Dis is a daughter?"

Had she not absorbed her Valentine's Day birth? Did she not recall my occasional role as poop-fairy concerning her diapers? No, she was probably infant-thinking "from each according to his ability, to each according to her need."

But her Sherlock talents were crucial in unlocking the mystery, of which more later.

Dooie was her mother's child. Dorothy, Dooie, Dooie-ooie, was embraced by Deirdre's healing circles. The tiny mite that grew into a leggy fairy child, vivid, blind, deaf with love. What exquisite hands she would have had if she hadn't gnawed her nails.

Tertullian she was not, but she did go along with her mom's *Credo quia absurdum est* doctrines. I suppose faith has a place in this world, but certainly faith *in* the world and its workings is misplaced. I hoped Dooie's edenic innocence would mature enough to smell the difference. Otherwise it would be a life of "Want some candy, little girl?" or later, "How'dja like to come up and see my etchings?"

What was most interesting to me was that for this lissome child, only the infinite seemed to suffice. The pandemic reed of humanity for the finite, the "all" that can be envisioned, understood, embraced, coerced, devoured — that world she ignored. Children of her type must dream up pure philosophies, but hers was so pure, she could never imagine corralling it in articulate form.

She was a powerhouse nonetheless. The Little Cloud Girl in her light dress, leaning over the banisters, as Joyce put it, listening. It was a gift to be so listened to.

The Sisters Hyde: body, mind, and spirit. How can a dad go wrong?

On the other hand, from fourteen on, some fathers might observe that they were becoming hot little bitches, the admission of which is *verboten*, but which phenomenon is widely felt, and too often acted upon. They are children, and yet not children. Consider: Juliet was thirteen when Romeo climbed her balcony and spent the night. Beatrice was nine when Dante first fell for her. What is the Mann Act compared to the act of love — love I said — not lust. What statute really understands "statutory rape"?

It is true that singly, doubly, or à trois, all of them turned eyes wherever they went. And not just male eyes, since, seeing them, younger women sweetly remembered their youth, and mature dames detested them for the reminder. But male eyes *were* the bigger problem.

At that age, the genitals seek one another in a grave,

sweet dance — oft suffused with ethanol — and then young souls, shallowly connected, believe they have "found" one another. And of course young ladies, Proust's *jeune filles en fleur*, are most delectable in those years, feeding themselves on pap for the heart. And so to achieve balance, and according to the law of Action and Reaction, young men are maximally detestable.

There is not a young girl alive in whose secret (developing) breast, the premonitions of passion are not stirring — sniffing what they suspect as the essence of existence, for only (so says the pap) a woman who loves is truly a woman. Perhaps some pure, childlike mind like Dooie's may ignore the premonitions for a while and will not, in this budding stage, yearn to imbibe the sweet mystery. But even her time will come, and for each of the Oooies, come it did, and hard.

There was nothing I could do. There they stood, sauntered, danced, triplets of war, and daughters to be wooed. Their childhood stupidities — touching a hot stove, or eating shoe polish — were behind them. On to stupidities bigger and better.

My debut as enraged father came first of course with Cooie, my oldest, Daddie's pet, the Wittgenstein-weeper.

"Once and for all, I will not allow any hot-shot college boy to trespass on your private zones. You will guard them — or I will guard them for you. I shall break that handsome face into a thousand pieces if he puts it where it doesn't belong. I'll beat the crap out of him and after that turn him over to the police for statutory rape."

Her response? "Fuck you, dear father."

It was an eye opener.

On the other hand, taking Looie to the woodshed was all too familiar. I prefaced my remarks with a comment on her current "existentialist" male attire which screamed "to hell with you" to all and sundry.

"Is this what the fashionable protester is wearing these days? What are you up to, organizing for the ethical treatment of black snakes?" She ignored the comment. I continued with careful introductory prose.

"You are, it seems, very much in love, and, as you may have come across in your study groups, in that situation, everything seems beautiful."

"To those who are liberated."

"Yes. But as an old practitioner of maledom, I am not entirely convinced as to the faithfulness of your beau."

She, of course, could smell advice coming from a mile away, so I was forced, once again, into self-defeating expletives.

"If he ever seriously touches you, I'll contrive to have him killed, and sent directly to his maker. And of course, if you disobey me, I'll cut you to ribbons, with a spanking the like of which no one has ever seen. Do you really think you live in Paradise where death does not sting?"

You can imagine how effective this conversation was. Afterwards, it was I who broke down in tears, I, the soft slob of the world.

But the hardest encounter of all was with Dooie, a victim of her sentimental education, swooning at the time over a currently unnamed swain. Was it Moishe's 22-year old, whom we had briefly met at a tailgate party on the lot? The Boss's son? Could be worse, except that he was a gangly, grasping lout, entirely without the oddball charm of his father.

No doubt she was passionately in love, swearing her eternal pearls off onto a swine, whoever he was. I could feel her being corrupted minute to minute. For all her naiveté, and perhaps because of it, she was a real adventurer in life. And wherever she trod, she trod passionately, blindly, in search of hidden wonders. I could imagine all the unintended promiscuity in her mind, all the unformed determination not to be left out of the party, not to miss out on being tromped on, or being left blind, miserable, and naked. Woe, woe will be unto her, the most woe of all.

But could I yell at her, trample her blossoming flower? No. The best I could come up with was to warn her against any unladylike intoxication in mixed company. (Meanwhile, loyal spirit, pure soul, make the most of your delusion. You don't stand a chance, but take it anyway.)

She readily agreed.

Thus, the Hyde pentagram, with Deirdre and me at the bottom, and the Sisters Hyde arcing over us on top. A star family in the fallen terrestrial world.

One more short, but poignant family story.

It was inevitable that existentialist, now beatnik, Looie took to and espoused as gospel Allen Ginsberg's *Howl*. The best minds of her generation and all that. Allen had been a student a few years after me at Eastside High, "Home of the Mighty Ghosts". That's us, Allen and me, go Ghosts!. By the late fifties, I was too old and bourgeiosedly engaged to become a beatnik, but I did undertake an extensive reading of my fellow Ghost, a study which predated Looie's black beret by several years. So I always had that ace up my sleeve to defend myself against her accusations of being square.

I found Allen's poetry to be paranoid in part, but it also addressed political issues I myself had been concerned with. Erotic, to be sure, but meditative, out to explore every aspect of human experience he could get his hands on or his penis into, no matter how messy, or to me, unpleasant. I give him credit for that.

I mentioned in passing that our family doctor, the one who pronounced our babies well, was a Dr. Williams, Dr. Bill to us. It was only in reading Ginsberg that I discovered how important our doctor was to American literature. Who would have guessed? *The* William Carlos Williams.

In the introduction to the poem "Death News", written on Dr. Bill's death in 1957, Allen recounts a pilgrimage made to the deathbed by himself, his lover Peter Orlovsky, and the poet Gregory Corso. They asked him if he had any wise words to impart before he bowed out. Our beloved old doctor raised himself up on one elbow, pointed out the window curtained on Main Street, and croaked, "There's a lot of bastards out there!"

One of them must have been me. He wanted to practice among us.

8. EYES ON THE PRIZE

Back in '56, Moish had mentioned, I thought as a joke, that he would be running for president. In fact, he even called a lunchtime lesson on "Leadingship", and we all thought it would be about how salesmen had to lead their customers toward and into a purchase, or perhaps how we should all take some kind of leadership role as citizens of Paterson, roles which would not only serve the city and our collective self-esteem, but would shed some ancillary publicity on Madman Moishe's Deals on Wheels. We thought he might even provide us some tricked out campaign cars with his cartoon self painted on the doors. Or Shriner go-karts and fezzes.

The meeting came to order, and I took notes, so we could hold him to whatever silly proposals sprouted from the top of his crazy-haired head. Ed, Bud, Al and I sat around the "lesson table" in Moish's office. On the outside door , a big sign read OUT TO LUNCH — which we all, and probably all of Paterson, knew had multiple meanings, some unintended. But today's sign had been revamped in red, white, and blue.

He opened with a stunner:

"OK, I know de answer to det before you even esk de qvestion."

Question? What question? We didn't even know what this meeting was *about* other than leadership skills.

"De answer is det dis country has a little problem vit marbles in de head."

"What is that the answer to?" Ed asked.

"Vhaddya tink, dummkopf?"

We sat there, blank.

"De qvestion is vhy I should run for President, vhat else?"

"You want to run for president?" I asked. "Against Eisenhower? Against Stevenson?"

"Vhat, you like Ike, you like de Egghead? You vant a president who plays gulf all de time? You vant a president who sasys big voids and has holes in his shoes?"

It's true, Eisenhower didn't come across well on television. Four more years of that grinning skinhead might send me to Canada. His veep Nixon was a crook too obvious to mention. And Stevenson was seen as hoity-toity snob by middle Americans, and even by me. And Khrushchev didn't have to bury us. We were already doing a good job of burying ourselves under a shitload of atomic waste and red-baiters and plastic radios. We were the enemy, not the commies, and somebody ought to say that. But would it be Moish?

"Dis is Amerika," he raged on. "I yem a citizen. I yem qvalified to run — I looked it up in de Voild Almeneck."

"Are you really a citizen?" Bud asked. "I thought you came from…"

We all realized that none of us had any idea *where* Moish came from.

"I came from, I came from. I came from *sumvhere* — just like you. You kin run for president, I kin run for president, except I'm smarter."

I raised my hand, as we were permitted to do in lessons, and, after waving it like in the second grade, I was called on.

"Boss," I asked, "Since when are you interested in social questions, in the world outside Meshugeneh Moishe's? I thought you were fixated on growing this lot, maybe putting Paterson on the map as the center of used car sales in the northeast. Now all of a sudden you're into Faustian discontent, and desire to reform the world?"

"Don't give me vit your intellectual business. Vhat's wrong vit reforming de voild? Reforming de voild means better business for Moishe's. We reform it in *dis* direction. If I'm president you make more seles, you make more money. You hev a problem vit det?"

"No, no, I…"

"You tink you're so smart? You tink de preests know from education? Det's a laugh. You don't know your punim from your pupik. If, Moish, de most successful person in Paterson, de most successful person in Paterson from all time, maybe de *only* successful person in Paterson of all time, kent be elected president, who ken? You tink de public vants to support det cream puff just because he invented e Eisenhower jacket? My tailor is better than his. Or det omelet-head? Vhat kind of a name is Adlai? Vud you buy a car from someone named Adlai? So who is left? Me, det's who."

"Will you run as a Republican or a Democrat?" Bud asked.

"I vill run as a Me."

"But you have to be chosen at one of the conventions. Republican or Democrat."

"Vy I kent have my own convention? Dis is a free country, no?"

We all looked around at one another. Where to start? Actually, I didn't know how the convention system got started, or even the Republicans and Democrats. What did they have to do with Whigs and Tories?

"Vhere are dese conventions?" he wanted to know.

Al was our political go-to.

"The Democrats are in Chicago at the International Amphitheater, and the Republicans in San Francisco, at the Cow Palace."

"I am not a cow, so I vont be a Republican. On de other hend, a palace... I'll tink about it. Vhat's de difference between dem, de Republicans and de Democrats?"

Al again: "The Democrats are for the little man, and the Republicans are for rich people."

"How liddle is liddle? You mean like midgets?"

"No, no. Little guys like us."

"Us? You tink I'm liddle?"

"No. I mean average Joes…"

"My name is Moish. You know vhat dat is from? Moses! You tink Moses vas an average Joe?"

"Sorry. It was just an expression."

There was an uneasy silence for a minute while Moish considered and we floundered. What would this madness mean for us, for the lot, for our jobs?

"Vhen are dese conventions? Ken I be in both?"

"I doubt they'd let you be in both. They're sometime in August."

"Dey vouldn't let me? Who vould stop me? Vhen in August?"

"Third and fourth weeks, I think," Bud offered.

"It's too hot. My vife doesn't like to leave her air conditioning. Maybe I vait till next conventions, when I hev time to make a pletform vid Commandments. If de president doesn't make Commandments, nobody vill believe he is a president."

"Presidential," I said.

"Det's vhat I said. And de foist commandment is 'You Heve To Heve Presidential Campaigns In De Vinter — In Florida.' Everybody knows det. Cless dismissed."

What got into him? America?

I don't think I really described this strange man the first time round. How old was he? To which question, he would invariably answer, "Old." He had no beard, for as he often said, "Better a Jew vidout a beard than a beard vidout a Jew," the implications of which, being Catholic, I never really understood. But could he have even grown a beard if he wanted to, and what color would it have been — who knows? We didn't even know if he had hair or not, because we never saw him without his fright wig, which he justified as being part of his brand. "It shows off my face," he announced. With his crazy gold hair and significant teeth, and the twisted disarrangement of his features when he laughed, he might have been God or Satan or the Ancient Mariner or simply some dangerous lunatic for all we or anybody knew. Some brand!

And the laugh. He laughed a lot. Except when he was ominously sullen. And he laughed so cacophonously, so hysterically, so from-head-to-heels, with such deep-from-the-gut bellowing, we were afraid he would shatter the showroom windows. Customers would flee, but he would coax them back, heve pity on me, with eyes streaming. And some did take pity on the poor, lovely, so-happy-funny man, and returned entirely buttered-up.

Man has been called The Laughing Animal (if you discount apes and hyenas), and Carlyle, for one, thought you could learn a lot from how a person laughed:

"How much lies in Laughter: the cipher-key, wherewith we decipher the whole man! Some men wear an everlasting barren simper; in the smile of others lies a cold glitter as of ice: the fewest are able to laugh, what can be called laughing, but only sniff and titter and snigger from the throat outward;

or at best, produce some whiffling husky cachinnation, as if they were laughing through wool; of none such comes good. The man who cannot laugh is not only fit for treasons, stratagems, and spoils; but his whole life is already a treason and a stratagem."

But what were we, what was anyone, to make of Moishe's unrestrained, maniacal, barely human, perhaps superhuman guffaw descending from some great and terrible height and simultaneously welling up from an equally inconceivable abyss?

And the laughter, the presence or absence of his ferocious jolliness, was merely a corner of the daily weirdness he visited upon his little plot in Paterson.

His vulgarity knew no bounds. He was constantly picking his nose as a kind of grooming, and flicking away the results. When he wasn't picking, he was blowing it with the sound of an elephant into a filthy red handkerchief he would cram between uses into his jacket pocket. But the worst was his spitting. Spitting, he explained, warded off bad luck, and the spit had to be in motion to be effective, so a symbolic, dry "ptui" just didn't make it. Most often he would spit into his handkerchief, but if the oncoming luck was really bad, it would be right on the showroom floor. Though we were the only business which still had spittoons in the 1950s, they were rarely used. And he wore a yarmulke.

Whatever his age was, he was satanically fit. While on the surface, he might have seemed just a queer little old man, he demonstrated a remarkable level of muscular activity, pacing with the restless walk of a madman. Sometimes the walk turned into a stalk, giving off a silent grimness. You never could tell what was going on, but it sure didn't seem normal. Meshugeneh Moish was a fitting, if inadequate, cognomen. Sometimes he would disappear into the basement of the dealership for the whole day, and none of us knew when he would emerge, or in what condition, or with what new plans he had for us, his minions. He was good Moish and evil Moish, but in any case, he was a splendid old geezer, not entirely fraudulent, and what more can anyone ask?

The fifties were the prosperous post-war years. The Eisenhower years. We had bombed our foreign competitors to bits, the G.I. Bill was producing an educated workforce, and dumb old Ike was smart enough to keep much of FDR's public busy building the interstates, as if to Moish's order.

See the USA

in your Chevrolet,

America is asking you to call.

Drive your Chevrolet

Through the USA

America's the greatest land of all.

Oil was domestic and cheap, and technical advances well-lubricated. And after saving balls of string during the depression, and having sugar and nylons rationed during the war, Americans gave themselves free-range license to buy,

buy, buy. And not just buy, but — driven by advertising — "buy now, pay later". The very first credit card appeared in 1950, and the rest is history. In fact, *history* was history — for most people, but not all.

Invisible in the glitz of chrome on cars and toasters were many poorer families with no purchase on purchasing. These were our customers at Moishe's, people awash in everyone else's momentum, but unable to afford their own. They, too, need transportation, but affordable, affordable. (Moish prohibited the word "cheap". "Cheep is for boids.")

So, with our eyes on a usually ignored market, MM's flourished and grew. "Deals on Wheels" — that's what they wanted, and that's what we gave them. And what deals! Sometimes the boss simply gave cars away. "Dey need a car, dey ken't afford one. So vhat are ve going to let them, sit around on dere tuchas and starve?"

Or he would often sell a car for one dollar. When the customer objected, Moish would come back with "OK, for you, two dollehs." And the customer would have to work him up from the bottom, but only to the low two figures. He'd become adamant after that. "Nineteen dollehs. Take it or leave it." They usually took it. And Moishe's fame spread.

If another car dealer came by, in disguise, to take advantage of the madness, or someone pretending to be down and out, Moish would tease out the truth, like Porfiry Petrovich stalking Raskolnikov. Somehow he could sniff the contents of a bank account down to the nearest dime.

Three factors kept Meshugeneh Moishe's from plummeting into the arithmetical abyss implied by his lose-as-much-money-as-possible business plan. The first was the boss's uncanny ability to come up with high quality, low-mileage, well-maintained used cars from God knows where. And only God knew what he had paid for them. Some were the mythical "used by a little old lady just for church" models. If within a hundred miles of Paterson, one of the guys would bus out to pick it up. But most seemed to arrive by truck, late at night, and there they were on the lot when we'd get into work. First thing in the morning, Moishe would tour us through the new acquisitions, their problems and their wonders.

The problems were few, thank goodness, since early on I, with my mechanic's background, was the entire service department. Later, as business became more than brisk, we hired another two mechanics, and I graduated to a more exalted sales & service manager.

And I have to say that *I* was the second major factor keeping this oddest of businesses afloat. If Moish was the bright, benevolent yin, I was the dark, malevolent yang, making sure that, behind Moish's back, or to his blind side, we squeezed every nickel out of every customer, no matter his or her or their financial status.

Being beyond good and evil has its uses, and being relatively charming and handsome was particularly useful with women customers or couples. It may seem boastful to say, but I, Charlie Hyde, may have been the first second-wave feminist. A decade before Betty Friedan, I set out to make MM's the most female-friendly car lot in town.

Buying a car, especially a good used one, is often uncomfortable for women, who have been trained to give the auto-world over to the men in their lives. I alone at MM's seemed to understand how important women are in family decision-making, (even though it was I who made most of my family's decisions to ward off Deirdre's astrological recommendations). So, with women or couples, I was particularly laid-back, consultative, and respectful, encouraging questions, and answering in feminine, less-than-assertive, but still professionally knowledgeable terms. It wasn't long before MM's was making more sales to women and couples, than any other lot in Paterson.

Equally important were some of my other stylistic and policy innovations. In spite of the fact that — as I have already reported — I was into gypping people for their own good, for their basic education in American values and mores, nevertheless, and equally important, was faking the appearance of honesty. Ours was the first, and for a long time, the only used car lot offering its customers up-front "no haggle" pricing, with window stickers listing the original retail price, the Blue Book price for the current model, and the Meshugeneh price, together with a subtraction for the innumerates about how much they were saving, and MM either making or even losing at its "stupid" prices. I put "no haggle" in quotes because sometimes there *was* haggling. but haggling downward as one of us tried to cinch a sale to up our statistics. Since Moish wasn't into maximizing profits, he rarely objected to this unique dynamic.

In spite of my mechanic duties reconditioning the few cars that needed some before sale, and my managerial duties overseeing the middle level of the operation, my sales statistics were markedly better than those of Ed, Bud, or Al — as you might imagine, having read their biographical sketches. I was simply smarter, quicker, more ambitious than all of them combined. I refused to even think about losing a sale, and it was rare when I did, and usually not my fault. For example, one gentlemen, reaching for his wallet to make a downpayment, discovered he had been robbed, and was without money or identification. Upon hearing that the family car would cost them just $8, one woman had an epileptic fit, and the medical dimension upstaged the sale, which was consummated only later. As I say, not my fault.

Overall, even with the relative sluggards on the sales force, the volume and tempo of sales grew and grew, and although the profit margin was small, all our bank accounts grew with it. But mine was definitely a crucial input, and my balance commensurate with the unimpeachable wisdom of "he profits most who bilks the best." Moish or no Moish, it's the American way. America will screw whomever it wills, when and how it wills, and will stop screwing them only when it is ready to stop. No infiltration from the edenic civilization of

Moishland can possibly transform this core national practice. As the good doctor Bill observed, we will always be a nation of bastards.

So — Moish's procurement skills and maniacal unbusiness sense, balanced by my fashioning a noble path of dishonesty were two huge factors that catapulted MM's Deals on Wheels to the top. But there was a third factor, hard to describe, and harder to account for. No matter what we did, things always worked out in our favor. As an experiment (I tried this only three times, but still…) over the course of a year, Moish had acquired only a few cars that needed any reconditioning. But you can't always tell. A slow head gasket leak may lead to a blowout. A transmission irregularity deeply buried in the gears may turn evil. A small flaw in the cooling system may overheat and destroy an engine. These were the three situations I let pass, just to see. And none of them, not one, led to a complaint. None of our cars were sold "as is". In fact, reconditioned or not, all of our cars had a six month or 3,000 miles guarantee, and an unsatisfied buyer had the option of returning the car for another or for a 110% refund on the purchase price. No one ever returned a car. Not one unhappy customer among the thousands we sold to. No one in this nation of mutually-screwing self-seeking bastards even bothered to trade back in for the 10% profit. How was it possible? *That* was the mystery, the mysterious third factor. It was as if there were a cloud of omnipotence hovering over 836 River

Street, and then again, after our move down the block, over to 754-794. Hard as I tried experimentally, in effect, we could do no wrong..

When I first became sales manager and was given responsibility for designing sales approaches, I used to stay in the office late at night looking out the window at the rows of shiny cars yet to be sold, wild with the desire to move them. Some of my best sales gimmicks came to me at night when I studied the assembled ranks of tops and hoods. When I'd come home late, having missed dinner, it was hard to convince Deirdre that I wasn't secretly seeing another woman. But I wasn't or only very occasionally, and that, with the private agenda of selling her a particularly expensive car.

My inner H (the Heidegger and Hrothgar one) would triumph, refurbishing the lot, translating M's tactics of miracle, mystery and authority into my own trinity of magic, mystification and tyranny. I studied every book on the history of advertising in the Paterson Public Library, and spent occasional evenings in similar searches at Rutgers. Moishe's statue with its lottery pattern of lights had ceased to draw crowds. I must have been possessed by the devil when I hung a cage from a cantilever off its shoulder, and paid a series of down-at-the-heels actors to do "happenings" which would increase attention. That month of attractions earned us an illustrated article in the *Tulane Drama Review* and seeded the beginnings of what is now acclaimed as performance art. One of the performers imitated Moish, yelling down to the public all the secret ways he (actually I) was cheating them. They loved it. Sales increased 35% in the days following his appearances. You can't tell anyone anything he doesn't already know. I tell them I'm cheating them (they laugh), and hey, we're used car dealers. Do they need to know more?

And how did car dealerships ever function without Muzak, the most world-changing invention preceding the atom bomb? I installed a high-end tape recorded system with speakers from the statue directed into and beyond the lot playing treacly ambient music, featuring strings with sporadic harps and chimes. The Christmas spirit all year round, more than Christmas, more heavenly, less jinglebellsy, music to inspire Gustav Mahler.

And bright lights. While most people became depressed, we eagerly awaited the days getting darker to transform Meshugeneh Moishe's into the brightest spot in Paterson, possibly in all of New Jersey. The city's hopelessness quotient went down. I measured it myself with random surveys taken in the winter with summer surveys as controls. I admit to frequently indulging in the lie statistical, but the research was for real.

Sometimes I felt like Pogo, "confronted by insurmountable opportunities". But I overcame them all with new ideas brought forth by our night lights reflecting off our cars, and utilizing early morning teeming-brain alpha-states. The rules were yet to be written, and my car lot world became a glorious jumble of liberatory lawlessness. The AAA even put us on New Jersey maps as a state "attraction".

Money poured in as if we were a financial arm of Paterson Falls. We were all — I more than the others, and God only knew about Moish — getting rich. Concerning which, I've done some honest reflection: It is no mortal sin to be poor, but neither is it one to be rich. I don't mean rich like that gangrenous tribe that has all the money now, staring dead ahead, completely blind, pitiless, empty of grace. Georg Grosz nailed them, and Bruegel the Younger before him. But I must be honest: I am drawn to the adornments of the earth — such as spectacular cars. I enjoy the joys of the world. Is that a crime?

We all secretly understand that Hobbes was right, and acknowledging that, I have derived my moral code from the *bellum omnium contra omnes*, the war of all against all. I have my own form of morality — passionate, imaginative, and sophisticated. And in doing so, I become part of the great brotherhood, not just the brotherhood of H, but the Brotherhood of Man, a member of that all against all in the universal bond of guilt which has reigned since the appearance of apples and snakes.

Like my namesake, I am doing my own version of Dr. Jekyll's experiment, an attempt to attain honest purity and power over self. As a society, we have learned to obey. It is now time to learn to command, and particularly to command ourselves.

Like Edward Hyde, my instincts are strong, and now making an undisguised detour through my bank account. With Jefferson, I submit that the pursuit of happiness and the avoidance of pain is the center of practical wisdom.

Can I be more honest?

I have forthrightly described my thinking, my feeling, and even my intuition about these things. Yet Jung reminds us that there is a fourth psychological function equally important: judgment. And although I think these things, feel them, lust for them, I also judge them. And so, let me enlighten you with my

SECOND ANALYTICAL INVECTIVE
Judgments on Self and Wealth

As wisdom has it, win a little, lose a little. Or as greater wisdom might have it, win a lot, lose a lot. With all this gain, what is lost?

First, as St. Paul would have it, *caritas*, empathy, compassion. Since the rich and powerful have little worry about the kinds of threats common people experience, they can easily ignore them, and the people that experience them. Yes, "uneasy lies the head that wears a crown." But that's nothing a couple of bodyguards and a good sleeping pill can't deal with.

Second, and related, is the loss of humility, of "'umble" as Uriah Heep would style it. More money, more power = more aggression. Enough is never enough, and as pushback builds with a growing sense of injustice, pushforward grows to counter it. The urge for a quantitative edge grows into a need for a qualitative edge, and to this, there are no limits.

And then, one can count on a decay of ethics. All's fair in love and war, is it? So it is in business, calculative thinking, and cost-benefit analysis. Even in Paterson, we notice that people driving the most expensive cars are less likely to yield right of way, and more likely to cut in front of other drivers and pedestrians. The Golden Rule subjugated to the rule of steel (and gold).

All this is self-reinforcing. That the more you have, the less you want is a schoolgirl fantasy. The more one is paid, the more his time is "worth", and the more his self-esteem is linked to that number. It's even more true of power. Mercy does not grow alongside. Wealth and power are addictive. But there are no 12 step programs to contain them.

Finally, because the wealthy and powerful minority is generally perceived as evil by the far weaker majority, we superiors find ourselves traversing an adversarial world, adrift among the Enemy. This is not a healthy state of affairs. There are a lot of bastards out there.

Nevertheless, we pursue wealth and power regardless of the losses, and damn the torpedoes, full speed ahead. Even Meshugeneh Moish.

Unbelievable, unexpected, but in the late spring of 1960, he approached me as follows:

"Chollie, you a good boy."

("Uh-oh," I thought. "Something's up.")

"It's time again. I hoid it on de television."

"Time for what? You heard what on television?"

"It's time for me to run for President again."

"The television wants you to run again?"

"Yes, of course."

"But you didn't run last time."

"Det's why dey vant me to run again."

"Why?"

"Vhy??? Vhy you tink? De Russians are spootniking, dey're making a gep in de missles. Dey're making footsies vit de hippies in Cuba…"

"So you're going to run to beat the Russians? But *you're* Russian…"

"Det's vhy. You tink an Irish like Mr. Kennedy or a crooked like Mr. Nixin knows how to fight vit de Russians? Me, I know."

"How?"

"Don't vurry. I'll figure it out. It's a state secret."

I plopped down in a chair, dumbfounded.

"Look," he said, "I made you seles menager, right?"

"Right."

"And you're a good seles menager, right?"

"Better than good."

"OK. Better den good. So I vant you should also be my campaign menager."

"But I don't know anything about politics," I said.

"You know more den I do. Tvice as much, maybe tree, four times."

"I can't do that, and also manage the business."

"Feh, which is more important, used cars or de fate of de voild? I'll make Al de manager. Or Bud. Or Ed."

"They'll run Meshugeneh Moish's into the ground."

"So? You hoid of de resurrection? Go read your bible."

His arguments were actually unanswerable. But he was nuts.

The summer was spent preparing him for the convention and the debates, all of which he was sure he could get into because this was America, he was "eligible" and he had read it in the almanac. He thought it was his turn. And he knew he could win.

OK, but what about me? My payday consisted of a manager's salary, plus a commission on my sales. Given my skills, the latter far exceeded the former. If my salary transferred over to being his campaign manager, and without commissions, my family and I would starve. Growing girls eat more than little ones, and have developed articulated "needs".

I asked the boss what would happen to my commissions if I took on the campaign manager job for six months.

"If I vin, I make you rich beyond your vildest dreams."

"You don't know how wild my dreams are."

"Filty rich is good enough? Discustingly doity filty rich?"

"You're in the right ballpark."

"OK, it's a deal. If I vin, you become discustingly doity filty rich."

"But this is like a horse race. You have to give me odds."

"I don't know boopkis from horse racing, but I see you don't tink I'm going to vin. Dis is not a good attitude for a campaign meneger. Tell de trut. Vill I vin?"

"I doubt it."

"How many votes I vill get?"

"Realistically?"

"So vat else?"

"I don't know…eight, maybe, from the boys and our families."

"And me. I vote, too. And my vife."

"So ten."

"Ten is good. Ten is a minyan, but not enough so I become president."

"Right."

"Can you make me more than ten?"

"Maybe. Twenty?"

"You get me tventy votes, I only make you plain rich."

"Thirty, then?"

"Toity votes, doity rich only."

I was beginning to catch the hang of the haggle.

"Forty?"

"Forty … doity filthy."

"Fifty?"

"Fifty votes or more, discusting, doity, *and* filthy rich. And det's it. Det's my lest offer."

I actually got him to put it in writing even though his signature was atrocious.

"If Charles Hyde, my campaign manager, gets me fifty votes or more in the 1960 US election for president, I promise to make him disgustingly, dirty, filthy rich within the ensuing two years." (I thought it wise to provide a time frame.)

He signed it "Moishe". I said there were a lot of Moishes. He said he wouldn't get confused, he knew it was him. I asked him to sign his last name. He wrote "Meshugeneh Moishe." I told him "meshugeneh" wasn't a last name, it was an adjective. He said, "OK, den Meshugeneh is my foist name, and Moishe is de last. You heppy?"

It was hopeless. I had Ed and Bud sign as witnesses. They thought the whole thing was a riot, and were happy they would absorb my car sales.

Was *I* happy? It must have been clear, even to Moish, that if he could possibly win, or even get on a ticket, or even receive an answer to any query — none of which he could do — that *I* was not the one to get him there. He was quick to post a reward for the 50 votes he would accept — instead of the 100 million votes he would really need — as a winning effort on my part. So something else was going on. What? He seemed determined to "reward" me for something; and my being his campaign manager was as good an excuse as any to bring his Mr. Mxyzptlik shennanigans to a somewhat wider audience, maybe boost sales, and have his own kind of lunatic fun while doing it. But with respect to me, he surely had something up his sleeve. I could see it in his eyes.

When I came in the next day, there was a large sign hanging from the statue: MOISHE FOR PRESIDENT NATIONAL HEADQUARTERS. In smaller letters, "Sign my petition for entering to maybe win a free car. A good car, too. Not just junk." A potential candidate would need 1000 signatures from NJ voters who were members of the appropriate party. But he didn't know what party he wanted to be president of, so he picked Independent, first because you only needed 800 signatures, and second because independence was good, like the Declaration from Independence.

I told him I thought more than 800 people would sign up just to try to get that free car, and that he was a marketing genius, and he jumped up and down, victory achieved.

What I didn't tell him was that the filing deadline had already passed, and that state officials would not accept the signatures no matter how many he got. But why should I? Why not go through with the charade? He would interpret all the people signing up to win a car, a good car too, not just junk, as votes for him, I would be credited with way more than fifty votes gathered, and he would have to honor his pledge — signed and witnessed — to make me dirty, filthy, disgustingly rich.

But whatever my prize might be, I wanted to earn it

honestly. So I boned up, and developed a civics 101 course in which even Moish could get an A. At our first sit-down, before I could even get a word in, he warned me,

"Stop already vit de criticalness. I vant good suggestions how should I win."

"I'm not being critical. I…"

"Vhy not? I pay you to be my campaign meneger, you gotta voik for your gelt."

"OK, well let's start with the question of why you are running. You'll have to tell people."

"Vhy I'm running? If I don't run, everybody vill be afraid dey might hev to. De only ting we hev to fear is fear, right?"

"But don't you want to achieve something positive, something that no other candidate is proposing? You have to explain precisely what you intend to do."

"Sure. I vant people should stop running around like chickens vitout de head."

"So what would you do about it?"

"Don't vorry, I'll do something."

"Like?"

"Like I vould discourage anybody else from trying to be president. People are allowed to run, but they should stay home and take care of business and de children. And den I'll heve less competition, and be able to devote all my energy to de space program and meking more beautiful bomb shelters vit sunlight and plents."

"But nobody except in Paterson knows you exist. You

need an image, something the public would like to think you are even if you aren't."

"So dey'll put pictures in de paper?"

"But the only way you can get into the big papers is to kill someone, or rob a bank, or get sued by women you've cheated on."

"You vant I should cheat on vimmen? I don't cheat. I tell dem I vant to be deir president, and if dey like vhat I say, dey vote for me. Vhy not?"

And so on and so on. Although with his car business he appeared to be some sort of Jewish Babbit, unlike Babbit, he said any weird thing you can imagine. Also many things you can't imagine. And unlike Babbit, when he got politically passionate, his reason seemed to come and go in shorter and shorter cycles. Sometimes when you listened to him, you felt like some poor creature abandoned on a floodplain of rationality. If you thought about the strange things he said, they were often deep, but it's hard to know how dependable his intelligence was, whether he was for real or nuts.

At times he went from Babbit to some Jewish version of Aristotle's great-souled man. Shtick, of course, is always a bit of a racket, and bigger-soul-than-thou was his shtick. Or if not bigger, completely other.

What, for instance, did he want to name his party (once I convinced him he should have one, and not just one with hats and ice cream)?

"De Absolute Dictator Party."

Why? "Because I vant to tell dem vhat dey should do to make a better country, vit no qvestions esked. De president is busy. Who has time for qvestions?"

When I told him that this was a democracy and Americans didn't like dictators, especially absolute ones, he said, "Det's because dey are not funny enough. Vas Hitler funny? Vas Stalin funny? Vhen I'm president, I vill dress all up in red, like Captain de Marvel. Den ve can have de Big Red Cheese Party."

Let us stop and think about these things. Was he saying that pitching himself as a potential dictator would make Americans think more deeply about the meaning of freedom? Was his dressing in red actually an end run around the House Un-American Activities Committee, preaching the vision of the New Man? You couldn't put anything past him.

His first campaign slogan summed it all up: "You vant to be bored, vote for anyone but me."

But as if this were not enough, there was a slogan a week, part of his "Dis Veek's Slogans" ads:

"Vote for me — I'm older den you."

"If you don't like me, vote for me anyhow. You might change your mind."

I told him he needed more positive slogans. He responded with

"Kvetching is not enough!" and "I'm for good and against evil. Vhat's so meshugeh about that?"

You may consider these the ravings of some crack-brained

old codger, but those cracks contained plenty of smarts. Moish, after all, in only a few years, starting with God knows what, had built the largest used car dealership in northern New Jersey. He'd reinvented car advertising, capturing "zany" for his own inimitable label, beginning with the huge statue of something like himself illuminating a whole neighborhood of Paterson, and randomly distributing gifts to its watchers.

"I'm for lots of stetues," he would say, "to remind people what a great country ve got."

He wanted to announce his candidacy at the Statue of Liberty, because it was hollow. Why? Because "You can valk up de stairs, and look down on all de huddled messes, and hock them a chinek to breathe as if dere free. It's inspirink." I convinced him to start local.

When I told him he needed some analysis of the country's problems, some positions his candidacy could take, you know, like

— What was his position on the Taft-Hartley Act?

— on atomic weapons?

— on organized crime?

— on containing the Soviet Union?

— Did he believe in civil rights?

— Who would he appoint to the Supreme Court?

In response, for a whole week his radio ads announced "Vhat dis country needs is a good 5¢ knish." And then Ed, Al, Bud, and I had to make and sell five cent knishes at the dealership for the next month, — potato and kasha both —

as if we didn't have other work to do. But he insisted his ideas be tested. Both browsing and sales did go up significantly.

When I pressed him on fitting more into the American historical presidential campaign tradition, he came up with "He'll Keep Us Out Of Normalcy" and "Tippecanoe and Moishe Too", the latter of which was surprisingly popular, spawning many handmade signs on the Rutgers campus, though I doubt the students knew who Tippecanoe was, or why.

But my favorite of his slogans, and deep it was, too, was "Moishe's Motto: STOP, LOOK, AND LISTEN. You never know vhen a train is coming," a notion with which one might surely live a constructive life.

To earn my keep as his campaign manager, I offered to write a stump speech for him. He refused, indignant. "I got vhat to say. You vant I should say your voids, not mine?" Instead I simply made him an outline of successful, wide-ly-used stump speeches: introduce yourself, thank the organizers, tell a personal story, why you are running, outline some issues that concern you, contrast yourself with your opponents, and say what you'd like your listeners to do if they want you to win.

And this was his version of my wisdom, as delivered and recorded in Roosevelt, New Jersey on July 4, 1960 to kick off his campaign. His voice was oceanic, and he needed no mike.

Hallo, all you liddle Roosevelts out dere,

It's Moishe here, come to see you on de fourth of July — you hoid of det date? —, and to tell you you should all vote for me for president of de United States. I'll keep dis speech short so you can get de knishes you really came for — only 5¢ — but my meneger tells me I should say tenks to de organizers — tenks for organizing dis relly, and making all dose signs and buttons I see vaving around. It used to be — back vid Mr. Vashington and Mr. Jefferson, ve hed soiten tings to debate, now we hev a vor vit buttons. But so ok. You got buttons. Kennedy buttons voises Nixon buttons voises de real Moish.

In spite of Roosevelt, New Jersey's radical political, cultural and architectural history, his audience had settled in, and straightened out over the new deal town's quarter century. One of 99 town-sized public works programs during the New Deal, it had begun as an agro-industrial, primarily Jewish, project to provide housing and jobs. Its residents would collectively own a farm and a factory, and live in homes designed by a young Louis Kahn and others in the Bauhaus style. Families paid the government $12/month rent for a new suburban home on a half-acre lot. Many residents came via ads in Jewish papers which advertised fresh air, sunshine, and a chance to garden. Tiny lower-east side masses yearning to be free. A new day ahead, hope in the hearts of Jewish men. So naturally everyone argued with everyone else. It may once have been the perfect utopian project for an erewhon speaker, but by the time Moish arrived, he was addressing a group of conventional business people and professionals out for some fireworks without the noise.

Dey call me Meshugeneh Moish because my car business is so von-derful — end you should see de prices. Ectually, I made up de name. But I'm not so meshugeh. You know vat is meshugeh, vat is de void meaning? (Cheers from the audience of landsmen.) *OK, you know vat is meshugeh, but do you know who is meshegeh? Huh? — You are, if you are tinking of voting for dose politicians to do your politics. You are all meshugeh.*

As Moish would say, "Oy!" What candidate begins by insulting his audience?

Vhat do you tink, just because you are already rich and famous, you have some special arrangement vit de future, it all comes out good? Even if you are all crooks and liars, you tink you ken trust even bigger gonifs to lead dis byutiful country?

The audience was beginning to wonder if this were such a fun way to spend the fourth of July after all.

But you call dis country civilized? Dey say Americans are still alive, so vhy do you ect like you're dead? I hear in Roosevelt New Joisey you all read highbrow megazines vidout pictures. So don't dey tell you about de real problems vhat is America? Vhat is dis here, crookedness vit big self-respect? Vhat's so respecting vit your vors on poor people, you sit around vatching eds on TV, and buying tschotkies vit your children becoming beatniks?

This last hit home for me.

Vhat do you loin from TVs? How to pick locks, how to hold up benks, vhich I edmit could be useful, how to kill people in very smart, expensive vays, how to get de laundry tvice as vhite, but tvice as vhite as vhat? I hope you're heving fun.

You tink de udder kendidates are going to do someting about all dis? Mr. Nixon, de crook who kent even get a good shave? Mr. Kennedy, de rich boy vit his entisemitic fadder end his glemourous vife vit her little pink hets? He's going to help de poor? You vote for dem, and a big darkness vill fall on all de lend.

My meneger tells me all of you in Roosevelt New Joisey are progressive. You all root for 1789, 1848, 1871, 1917, 1949, 1959. Vell, I vas dere, and believe me, it vasn't so great. So if you vant a real revolution vidout you hev buyer remorse, you got to do something more imprecticle. Are you so rich and heppy in Roosevelt New Joisey you become ungrateful, you just sit around? It's time to get serious and vote for me, Moish. Or at least write me some nesty letters I ken make fun of. De voild is only changed vhen people is villing to ect a little kukoo, more nuts den de politicians, or dey vill never go avay.

My meneger also tells me ve missed de deadline to get on de bellots. So you got to write me into de bellots, on de lest line. You ken just write Moish, M-O-I-S-H. If you tink dey vill vant two names (vhat's wrong vit one name?) put down Meshugeneh Moish. You ken figure out how to spell it, dey'll know who you mean. And det vay, even if I don't vin, maybe I'll sell more cars.

By de vay, if you need a used car, come over to Paterson. Ve got deals on vheels you'll never believe.

So remember, end dis is de toid time I'm telling you, vote for me, Moish. You'll be sorrier if you don't den if you do.

Having covered all the points in the successful stump speech outline, he started to leave, but was stopped by wild cheering.

OK, OK, tenk you, tenk you. Vote for me, and ve've got de famous Moishe knishes 5¢, at de table over dere. Buy lots of dem so ve cover our costs to get here from Paterson.

Improbable as it may seem, he did officially pile up 25,947 write-in votes nationally in the 1960 election. Look it up if you don't believe me. And probably more than that, since some of the more cantankerous election officials may have balked at grossly illegible handwritten or one-name entries.

And so I won my prize for getting him more than fifty votes. He had promised to make me "discusting, doity, and filty rich." Little did I know. But I am getting ahead of my story.

9. FILIAS MEAS

I mentioned that Moish's stump speech reference to the children of Roosevelt growing into beatniks hit home. Which brings me to the subject of my daughters, the Daughters Hyde — Cooie, Looie, and Dooie.

In 1956, they were 15, 14, and 13. And in 1956, there appeared on a Milton Berle Special, a 21-year old of questionable talent named Elvis Presley, singing a song called "Heartbreak Hotel".

He had long hair, chewed gum while he sang, so that you could barely understand him, slouched and scratched, bumped and ground (if that is the appropriate past tense of "to grind"), and during his appearance clowned and joked to the audience of sailors and their dates gathered on the deck of an aircraft carrier docked in San Diego. They must have been instructed to cheer and scream in appreciation.

According to him, he was lonely enough to die, or so he said, not because of his no doubt evil-smelling hairdo, or tasteless gangster clothing, but because his baby had left him (and who wouldn't?) So he had to become a bellhop or something at some heartbreak hotel, likely not frequented by the young Leona Helmsley. It was altogether ridiculous.

Thirteen-year old Dooie didn't know what to make of it all, and just sat there, expressionless. The year-older Looie was scornful of the white boy trying to get rich by imitating the music of poor Negroes. But my eldest, Cooie watched quietly until the last chorus, and then broke out in tears. "What's wrong, baby?" I asked her, and my use of "baby" triggered an even greater outburst of wailing. When Uncle Miltie moved on to the next act, and Cooie had quieted down, Deirdre asked more coolly than I "Why were you crying, dear?"

"He seems so lonely," she said. And she started to cry again. Tears for Ludwig Wittgenstein and Elvis Presley. It makes one wonder. I thought maybe she had just gotten her first period — something secret between mother and daughter I hadn't been privy to. But no. Apparently she wasn't alone in her concern, or uniquely sensitive. Over the next months, the papers and TV served up an unending series of stories and pictures of thousands, tens of thousands of teenage girls all across the country mobbing the poor singer, screaming and tearing his clothes from his back. He seemed to enjoy it. He certainly couldn't convincingly claim to be lonely enough to die.

After one of these child riots, some high Catholic functionary wrote to J. Edgar Hoover about the threat Mr. Presley posed to the country. "His actions and motions are such as to rouse the sexual passions of teenaged youth." Elvis was henceforth banned at our house after he autographed the belly and thigh of two enthusiastic young fans — right on TV.

The critics were in. The gray lady *New York Times* wrote that he had "no discernible singing ability," and identified his gyrations with those of "the burlesque runway." The *New York Daily News*, not the most highbrow of papers, announced that popular music "has reached its lowest depths in the 'grunt and groin' antics of one Elvis Presley. ... Elvis, who rotates his pelvis ... gave an exhibition that was suggestive and vulgar, tinged with the kind of animalism that should be confined to dives and bordellos". And unlike Uncle Milty, Ed Sullivan, whose own variety show was the nation's number one, declared him "unfit for family viewing".

But Dooie Hyde didn't read the *New York Times*, and Looie Hyde couldn't stomach its capitalist lies, and Cooie Hyde was, with tens of thousands of others of her national cohort, "in love with Elvis."

There was a good side to this. Presley brand low-class southern sleaze was unlikely to be equalled by any of the poor northern New Jersey slobs Cooie was likely to be approached by. Voltaire once noted that the perfect is the enemy of the good, and therefore of the much-less-than-good, and perhaps Cooie's mythic infatuation would protect her against local infestation. Or at least I hoped so.

Here, the Sisters Hyde were for once at odds. That Looie was so disdainful of Cooie's great love created an unwonted tension between them which poor little Dooie, quite over her head, had to mediate. But after a few months, her sweet sainthood knitted all together, and life returned to normal. Even Ed Sullivan decided that Elvis could appear on his show if he was shot only from the waist up.

Looie, too, had her music idols, but they were of the folk-singing and bluesy type, often black, with names like Blind Joe this and Howlin Sam that, and performing in clubs which didn't allow teenage girls. But Looie wasn't just a teenage girl, she had become an existentialist, and wore nothing but identical existentialist clothing day after day. Black skirt over black tights, black turtleneck, and an exotic black beret which she had gotten from no one knew where. Since she couldn't get into the bars, she spent her allowance and parental begging-bucks on Folkways records, folksong collections by another Moish, a Moses Asch.

I was quite relieved when by the late fifties, more white folk singers began to replace the Negroes in Looie's pantheon — Joan Baez, Woody Guthrie, Pete Seeger, the Weavers, Peter, Paul and Mary, the Kingston Trio. I'm not sure if the relatively upbeat young, white musicians really could ever replace those gnarled, lugubrious hands, and harsh, sad voices of the wretched of the earth in Looie's affection. A white negro at heart she was. But I was happy to be told that she was transitioning from being just an existentialist — which she said we all were whether we knew it or not — to being a beatnik, which I gathered meant an applied existentialist, whose existence preceded her essence, and needed some filling out for optimum worldview. She spent much weekend time commuting to and from Greenwich Village with a mixed crowd of similarly black clothed friends. I kept my fingers crossed, but they seemed a healthy enough New Jersey gang. None of them seemed up for suicide — which I was informed was the only really serious philosophical problem.

One of Looie's remarkable behaviors which she kept up from her pre-black-clothing days, was an interest in mysteries and true crime. Out of boredom with the traditional children's book twaddle, I had taken to reading Sherlock Holmes to the girls for bedtime stories. In spite of Deirdre's concerns, the crimes to be solved were not so horrifying as to yield nightmares, even in six-year old, emotionally fragile, Cooie. Little Dooie, at four, was barely interested, and worked on staying awake just to be part of the gang. But Looie, five, seized on the material with the sagacity of a serpent. She would out-Sherlock Sherlock, invariably coming up with the answers a few pages and clues ahead of him, though later, in a fit of Maoist self-criticism, she would observe that she often guessed, and that as Sherlock himself had opined in *The Sign of Four*, guessing is "a shocking habit — destructive to the logical faculty."

As she grew older, we supported her Sherlock mania, feeding her more and more volumes, including a facsimile edition of the original magazine stories from *The Strand*, with the now-classic Paget illustrations, from which drawings, minutely observed, she drew her own original conclusions.

Deirdre simply liked her being so smart, while I saw this Mozartian talent as leading to some really high-paying job which would keep her financially independent of whatever husband might be lucky or unlucky enough to grab her.

Along with her teen-silly study of Marx, Hegel and Proudhon, she also poured over volumes on handwriting analysis and phrenology, and examined her world with a Sherlocky magnifying glass, which we bought her as a joke, but which she treasured as a lens through which to view the world and gather its evidence. It helped that she was near-sighted. She also cherished a used book called *Language, Truth and Logic* which she had bought on her own, and I couldn't make head or tail of.

Over her cubby in the sisters' shared bedroom, she had, at 13, hung a sign reading "The emotional qualities are antagonistic to clear reasoning," which I at first took as a understated attack on her older sister, as well as a staking out of her own territory — until she informed me that it was another Sherlock quote from *The Sign of Four*, which I gather was her favorite story. "Novel," she corrected.

Again, this attachment had both a back and a front. On the one hand, it concerned me that she might be attracted to her hero's well described drug habits, and Deirdre was concerned that her passion for non-passion, might affect her emotional life. But on the other hand she'd be a harder catch for the pimply boys, and perhaps a tamper to Cooie's too urgent, tear-pumping heart.

As you shall see, all these qualities, talents and deficiencies would come in handy.

About little, now not so little Dooie, there is so much to say, but so few words with which to say it. She was dragged along in the tail wind of her older sisters, entranced with the improbable, but too predictable, marriage of Marilyn Monroe to Joltin' Joe Dimaggio, a husband in the Sicilian mode. For her, they were the best athlete and the prettiest girl, the homecoming king and queen of America. In that January of 1954, she was eleven. What did she know?, As instructed by Ike and her anti-Communist representatives in Congress, she added "under God" to the pledge of allegiance she had already memorized. I, myself, wasn't so sure of God's governmental status, but this was a battle I chose not to fight. Our Paterson schools were already integrated, and the girls had colored friends, but they had been wide-eyed at the cov-erage of the Little Rock riots of a few years ago, and now the articulated rise of negro militancy. Dooie at seventeen thought particularly funny Dick Gregory's quip, "Wouldn't it be a hell of a thing if this was burnt cork and all you people were being tolerant for nothing?" Her taste, I suppose, for the realities hiding behind the visible. She also thought hilarious (and trashy) a New York Times ad placed by the minister of some big church on Fifth Avenue, which she clipped and taped to her cubby: "For a spiritual lift on a busy day, DIAL A PRAYER. Circle 6-4200. One minute of inspiration in prayer." She and the sisters worked up a great performance in three-part harmony of the juke box hit, "The Man Upstairs":

Have you talked to The Man Upstairs?
'Cause he wants to hear from you!
Have you talked to The Man Upstairs?
He will always see you through!

For an encore, they would swing into "The Big Fellow In The Sky". Were such Hyde Sisters the good Catholic girls we had brought them up to be?

You can imagine how deeply that little fourteen-year old was affected by Sputnik. She had to watch it in every clear night sky. She made me buy a short wave radio so she could listen to its beeps. As Cooie had embraced the lonely Elvis, so Dooie gave her heart and soul to little Laika, the first animal in space, the poor stray dog cruelly suffocated as planned when her oxygen supply on Sputnik 2 ran out. Laika was Dooie's introduction to the abysmal tragedy, the massive moral failure underpinning life, that sweet little mongrel, sacrificed by science to advance human knowledge. Though the hubris was not her own, Laika the stray had strayed too far for her own good. For four years following her death, Dooie held a memorial ceremony in the back yard each November 3rd, among the falling leaves. Then she stopped.

These were our youngest's superficial traits. It was perhaps her lissome frailness, her fairy child heritage which gave her the firmest grasp on what I now understand were the deepest realities. And her nose for the unseen was as important as Cooie's urgings and Looie's forensics in solving the mystery which would beset us.

10. THE CONTRACT

O K. I, Charlie Hyde, he who is beyond good and evil, have put this topic off long enough. Classic French drama has the concept of the *scène a faire* — the obligatory meeting up, the crux of any story — and unfortunately, this is it. "Unfortunately", because a problem the Founding Fathers never imagined is that it would be only nut cases who ever try to run for president. And a *scène à faire* with a nut case is more problematical than most. Anyway, here goes:

On July 16, 1960, the day after John Kennedy, "de bootlegger's son", won the nomination at the Democratic Convention in the City of Angels, I found a note from MM in my mailbox at work. He wanted to have "a little talk" at lunch hour. While elementary school fears of being called to the principal's office are unworthy of a successful, mature man, still I counted the hours till his appearance at noon. After a general greeting, he crooked his finger at me, like the witch inviting the children into her lair, led me into his office, and shut the usually open door.

This was a fairly conventional 50s boss office — corner of the building, large windows, bookshelf with automotive literature, adding machine and intercom on blotter on large desk, a Jewish wall calendar for the year 5721 which each month commanded its viewers to STOP KVETCHING. The only odd thing in the room was a piece of (I suppose) art — a skewered porcelain sweet potato, very realistic. Moish's explanation, "It's not a sveet potateh, bubeleh, it's a yem — like I yem" — a gift given to him "by my vife on our nine hundret annivoisery." Fine.

He sat down in a customers' chair, and beckoned me to take his big boss seat behind the desk, an odd, though congenial beginning.

"So, Chollie," he began, "how's your life?" I'm thinking this could get weird. I've done my job, I thought, my sales were good considering the simultaneous campaign manager job, I'd gotten him far more than the minimum votes to qualify me for some kind of prize, and my knish-making had become excellent. I decided I had little to fear from this interview.

"You did good, Chollie. 25,947 votes is a lotta votes considering not everyvon hes a pencil. So…if you hed von vish for a revord, vhat vould it be? Vait, don't tell me, I bet I ken guess."

"What?"

"You vould like to get more rich."

"Yeah. Who wouldn't?"

"Some people vouldn't, but you aren't one of dem."

"I'd never turn down an opportunity to make a little more dough, that's true."

"And trut is good, right?"

"Right."

"Even if you hev to lie a liddle, right?"

My God, what was he thinking of? What did he know? My lies were no worse than his. Maybe a little less imaginative, but…

"Mote and beam," I countered, a little confused, though I thought he'd appreciate the biblical reference.

"Do you tink, Chollie, det udeh people exist?"

"Of course other people exist. If they didn't exist, why would we sell them cars?"

Was he accusing me of some metaphysical crime?

"How rich vould you like to get to get rich?"

"Well, I'd like to be a millionaire, like everybody else…"

"Everybody else isn't a millionaire, but you vould like to be one."

"Yes, sure. What are you getting at, boss? The way you are talking makes me feel as if I've missed doing something I should have done."

"Vhat if I promised you to be a millionaire?"

"How can you make that happen?"

"Don't vorry. I do it. A million dollehs. Every penny."

"And what do I have to do?"

"Just sell cars. You a good selsmen."

"A million dollars worth of commissions?"

"No commissions. You get to keep de whole price."

"Who pays for the stock, then?"

"Don't vorry. Someone vants a car, it's dere. New. And you get all de money."

"This is crazy. New cars cost 25 hundred dollars. To make a million, I'd have to sell four thousand cars."

"You'll sell four tousand cars. Eight tousand. Ten tousand."

"How will I sell eight thousand cars? No dealership…"

"Ten tousand cars you'll sell. You can sell for half price. Or less. Any price you vant. In two years you'll make a million dollehs."

"Where will the cars come from?"

"Don't vorry. Someone vants a car, it's here de next day. Any color dey make."

"Who makes? What kind of car?"

"Ford makes. Edsel is de car. Very edvenced. Lots of feechas."

"But nobody is buying Edsels. They're a joke, whatever features."

"At your prices, dey'll buy."

"Ten thousand will buy?"

"Ten tousand vill buy."

"So that's a million I'll make. But before taxes."

"Texes I ken't help. A million gross."

"OK, that's still a good deal."

"A kosher deal, de real ting from Meshugeneh Moish —
Deals on Wheels."

"Wait a second…why are you saying this?"

"Not saying. Doing."

"Why are you doing this?"

"Did you get me more den fifty votes?"

"A lot more."

"So now I will make you a lot more rich. Doity, filthy rich
like you sed. Vidout money, you kent take living for grented."

What did he mean by that?

"So now ve make a contrect?"

"What kind of contract? I thought you were just going
to get these cars for me, and I would make a million bucks."

"And vhen you make a million bucks, den vhat happens?"

"Then I'm rich."

"But you also hev to voik hard."

"I'm a hard worker."

"You hev tventy-four munts. Or you make a million
dollehs. Vichever comes foist."

"And then?"

"End den, you hev to do vhatever I tell you."

"Like what?"

"You'll know vhen I tell you."

"I have to sign an open-ended contract? Who does that?"

"You do. If you vant to make a million bucks. Vich you
do."

"What if you say you want all the money back?"

"Den det's vhat I'll say. But you vil already have figured how to cheat me and keep de money. I know you, bubeleh."

So it was to be a contest of wits. But I'd be starting out a million ahead. Lord, protect me from myself.

"OK," I said. "I'll sign."

He pulled an already typed contract out of his jacket. On it he promised to supply all the cars I needed for 24 months, and to ask no money from me in return. Also to do whatever I asked for for help, advertising, etc.

"You got a pencil?"

"Aha! Foist trick? Dis one you sign in pen."

He offered one. I took it from him, unscrewed the top, held it poised over the paper for ten seconds — and signed.

"You want a witness?"

"I'm de vitness. De oders shouldn't know vhat's going on. Dey veren't my menegers."

"Do I get a copy?"

"You don't trust me?"

What could I do but trust him and see what he came up with. If I didn't make a million in 24 months, I'd be off the hook for whatever, but I'd still be rich. The figure $999,999.99 glowed on my visual cortex. I got up, went for the door, and stopped.

"What's your purpose with all this?"

"Why should I have a poipus? I don't do poipuses.

"But you made this whole strange Meshugeneh Moish dealership. You must've had a purpose in doing that."

"I like doing. I do vhat I like, I like vhat I do. It's good-looking to me.

"But what does it mean, what you do?"

"It means. It means vhat it means. Why do you hev to know? I'm de boss. You don't like it?"

"No, no. It's just… To do so many crazy things…"

"So? You want I should do not-crazy tings? You vant I should be just like any udder boss? I don't treat you good? I yem vhat I yem, I do what I do."

"But there are rules, government rules about finances, taxes, about how you can treat employees."

"Govenment, shmovenment. You tink de govenment cares from you as much as Moishe does? You tink de govenment kin tell me how to run my business? I created all dis mishegas. I get to make de rules. If I didn't, I wouldn't be de boss."

"You give me the willies."

"End you give *me* de villies, vhatever de villies is. But *I* get to do someting about it. Vhat do *you* know? I vas doing dis before you vas even an itch in mommy and daddy's pupiks. Don't argue. Moishe knows best."

I nodded, turned, and walked into the showroom. The boys wanted to know what went on. I waved them off, just shaking my head. They thought they knew what that meant.

Was this whole contract thing just another one of his bossy ideas? Or was it more cunning than that? Surely he would be wanting to rake off some of the money flood I'd be bringing in. Maybe I'd figure it out tomorrow, but for now I suspected some kind of gyp. He thinks he's god around here? There must be stupid neighborhoods in heaven, too.

I went home early that day to tell Deirdre the news and discuss its implications. Though *I* see her almost daily, the reader has last encountered Deirdre as a young mother of three little girls. When I saw her that afternoon in July 1960, she was almost forty, and well-ensconced in her own domain, that of visionary homemaker with a sink full of garbage and grease, and a home which might have housed a poltergeist.

A few quotidian skills must have sublimated from her mind as well as her housewifery, likely liberated by too frequent consorting with the metaphysical. One of the properties of *homo sapiens*, at least female *homo sapiens*, seems to be an ability to believe in things that simply don't exist, or at least cannot be shown empirically to do so. Deirdre's adult world was a crude pottage of folklore and emotional quackery, populated with spells, charms, mantras, prayers, potions, and divine guidance unerringly received via purity of heart — fictions that I, at least, found wildly misleading or distracting.

Which is not to say that I didn't still love her, but at this point more as a curiosity than a partner. I would not drink her Tiger's Milk or partake of her Queen Bee Jelly. I did not worship the forever energetic Jack LaLanne as a health guru. I was not interested in ingesting "live-cell foods", since I definitely wanted all my food to be dead before I swallowed it. I abhored both cottage cheese and grapefruit, separately or in combination.

But though we inhabited separate, non-communicating worlds, and because I was not really fit for her companionship (or possibly any other), I continued to long for it. And so I shared with her, as best I could, my remarkable lunch meeting that day even though, being ignorant of Sir John Tenniel, she generally considered Moish to be Disney's inspiration for the Mad Hatter. Still, I was anxious to hear her reaction to her likely becoming the Mary Clark Rockefeller of Paterson.

She was beautiful still, though her indoor existence had made her stouter, and so pale that her lipstick seem to seethe upon her lips. Her black hair, like what was left of mine, showed streaks of gray. Each time I saw her in these days, I realized I had forgotten what she looked like. For some reason, it is hard to write about a wife. "Till death do us part, till death do us part" was all I could think of.

She surprised me with her first question: "Did you already sign the contract?"

"I did."

"In blood?"

"No, of course not. In Moishe's red ink from his 'let's make a deal' pen."

She sat at the kitchen table studying the bottom of her teacup as if to discern therein the meaning. There were signs everywhere for her, omens in the weather and the obituaries, in the birds and changes of season, and locally in the tealeaves in the cup. She seemed large with wisdom, or at least assertions.

"You don't have to believe me," she said, "but I understand things better than you. I get nervous when something bad is going to happen, and I am feeling nervous. This contract. Where it comes from. What it means."

"Aren't you happy? We may be getting very rich."

Somehow in this discussion, in her very own kitchen, she seemed like Shelley's moon, pale for weariness, wandering companionless, a river always flowing back into itself.

"We'll see what happens," she opined, and left the room. So much for delivering the good news. She had many fine qualities, but a sense of humor was not one of them. I was left to consider the affair on my own.

I would have liked to consult with Ed Dunnigan, my late father-in-law, but in case you're interested, he had recently become my late father-in-law, dying of "suicide" after being questioned by the Kefauver Commission. It was all very iffy.

So putting aside the fact that I had already signed the contract, I tried to "sleep on it" — which involved a sleepless night. What the hell was going on? Why did Moish come up with this scenario for me? What was he planning to demand when the contract was up, and would I be damned to accept the consequences? What could he afflict me with? Boils? A plague of frogs? And above all, who was this man, my boss, who was acting like some sort of a god? Moish 3:16. For God so loved the world that he came down himself and opened a used car lot in Paterson NJ....?

Yes, your Reverence, no your Highness, of course, I'll do whatever you say, your batshit lunatic Holiness, I'll even spend my days stinking up my office making knishes.

At the same time, there was something decidedly grave about Moish, something of huge dimension. He had scale. Overall, he was up to something in no way conventional, something ecstatically crafty, with more than a whiff of crime about it. The Victorians practiced high seriousness; Moish practiced a kind of low seriousness which is perhaps all the more serious for being low — at the level where it might take you out at the knees.

This business with the contract was the kind of deal you can imagine belonging to the Middle Ages. Jung thought that there were holdovers from other times walking around among us — Babylonians and Carthaginians and Middle Ages or Biblical types. Moish could be one of those, basically incomprehensible to us moderns, acting out some role from the childhood of the race. He certainly doesn't seem interested in Modernism, or Marxism, or any of those standard Jewish things. But, you know, without him, there would be nothing. I don't mean Nothing, Looie's turtlenecked *néant*. Just nothing, nothing interesting around here. He's really changed the world, at least in northern New Jersey — and beyond. I mean, at least 25,947 people with pencils were touched by him.

On the other hand, he's kind of deathy. Some people, even kids, are more full of death than others. He is very peculiar. On the other hand, who isn't?

Listen to me: "on the one hand", "on the other hand". He's got me talking like an old Jew already. But there is a lot of peculiar merit in some people.

What if he's wicked? I don't mean like a wicked witch, though he could be that, but more like a big Goebbels liar, up to some grandiose satanic scheme. No...I'll bet he's just trying to make a bigger buck off of me. All those extra sales he's talking about going through the office, but in my name not his? How much of an under-the-table cut is he taking? And what are the tax benefits?

Those kind of shysters have no friends. And who are Moish's friends? None. He has no friends, just customers, employees, "contacts". His wife never comes around. Is he disappointed in love? What kind of a person has a secret office in the basement? I could swear he's taller when he comes back upstairs. He looks like a sweet, crazy old uncle, but Duncan was right: There's no art which can find the mind's construction in the face.

Still I tried. I concentrated on the shifting expressions of Meshugeneh Moish, Moish the Most Odd. Whatever he would demand, I could just tell him off. I could make fierce, logical, poetic speeches full of classical quotations, infused with an evolved judgment, yet full of rage. Like Shakespeare.

But they wouldn't do a damn bit of good, would they?

I fell asleep around four a.m. The last conclusion I recall was "I don't know what this is all about, but it's happening."

11. EDSELMANIA

When I arrived at work the next day, there were two brand new 1960 Edsels in a prominent place on the lot. Tan and brown, aqua and white, they were by far the fanciest cars we'd ever displayed, and the only new ones. The used cars, even the Chryslers and Cadillacs, looked with covetous envy on the new arrivals. The cars looked like they were going 80, just standing on the lot.

Who ordered them? When were they delivered? This would become a pattern: some number of cars would arrive overnight, always unobserved, the noisy unloads unheard by neighbors. This was no Mafia operation. The papers were always in order, the VIN numbers kosher (there I go again), the odometers read 000 000.00. It was like loaves and fishes. The more the demand, the more appeared. By late spring, Moish had to purchase a larger River St. lot next block over to accommodate the Edsel Annex. Plus I hired a factory-trained Edsel mechanic to be prepared for the incoming service demands. But there were none. Zero. No cars came back, and there were never customer complaints, only hosannahs.

And I knew why. Because I took each of the first two cars to appear for a long test drive, the most grueling northern New Jersey could provide. No Rockies or Sierras here, no Mont Blanc, but there are some pretty steep hills around. And rural roads, and gravel, and good slick on that rainy summer day. Turnpike and traffic jam, sudden slowing and death-defying acceleration — those cars out-performed any of the thousands of vehicles I had driven. They were miracle machines. Here was Edsel Ford's design genius finally let loose from the any-color-they-want-as-long-as-it's-black legacy of his cantankerous old man. Cheers to Edsel's son, Henry II, who orchestrated this multi-gen Oedipal slaying of the deranged progenitor.

The interior smelled leathery as a shoe store. The design and engineering innovations were astounding. With no front posts for the curve-around windshield, there were no blind spots at crossroads. You never had to take a hand from the steering wheel to shift gears, as shifting was done by a set of push buttons in the wheel's recessed hub. The speedometer flashed red when you exceeded a speed limit setting, and the radio featured push buttons for favorite stations. The brakes adjusted themselves so that as the linings wore down depressing the brake pedal remained the same, and the parking brake was set by a foot pedal, and released with a dashboard control. There was tinted safety glass against the sun, wall-to-wall carpeting, generous contour seats with foam rubber cushions, tubeless tires, full-view turn indicators, warning lights for engine temp, and oil level. Driving fast, I couldn't hear the air rushing past. I felt like I was standing still, and the scenery was just running past the windows.

I'm starting to sound like an Edsel ad, but I suppose that's appropriate, since according to sales figures from Detroit, I soon became the largest Edsel dealer in New Jersey, then on the east coast, then nationally, and finally in the world. All from my ever-filled lot at 754-794 River St. The city of Paterson had to change the parking rules in the vicinity to accommodate all the shoppers, and the City Council was planning to add a light and left turn lane for Edsel-bound traffic. Though the factory-included license plate holders read MOISH AND HYDE EDSEL, the arrangements were entirely as promised. He stayed out of the business and out of my wallet, and helped wonderfully only as requested. Things grew like Jack's magic beans.

My sales prices began at 3/4 normal retail. But as demand grew exponentially, I knocked that down to 1/2, with well-publicized giveaways to charity and health organizations, and, using Moish's trick, to the random poor. I was not only raking in the cash, but also great waves of civic good will. I was constantly interviewed in the papers, including the *New York Times* and the *Wall Street Journal.* And not just in the business sections. *Life* magazine gave me a page, and *Time* featured me in some human interest story about the new entrepreneurs.

I could now afford to try a policy of "name your own price". What was shocking was that with rare exceptions of folks who might have gotten charity cars anyway, average Jane and Joes came up with figures higher than my current 1/2 price levels, which they didn't "think was fair to [me]."

Sales in 1961 were completely trippy. I thought it was just New Jersey with its feedlot of drug companies — Merck, Sandoz, Hoffman-Laroche, Bayer, Squibb, Wyeth, Johnson and Johnson smokestacks all blasting their particulates in the air between the Delaware and the Passaic rivers. Since the early fifties people had been popping Miltown as a tranquilizer now at the rate of a pill per second every day. It didn't keep them from going out to buy cars. (Did you know that Miltown was named after the town of Milltown, just east of the Jersey Pike?)

Earlier, it had been lobotomies — tens of thousands of them each year. But now, thankfully, the drug companies were acing out the surgeons. And speaking of Sandoz, what about that old Albert Hoffman, and his "medicine for the soul". For all I know, the entire New Jersey Turnpike could have been on LSD to account for our Edsel sales in '62.

There had been incipient madness in the air since the end of the war. What was it? The metastasis of super people in tights? Fluoride in the water supply? The hydrogen bomb? Photos of Auschwitz, TV ads like Moishe's, UFOs? Whatever was causing the epidemic, Moshe-Hyde Edsel was surely the benefactor. I myself was not immune. Even that first road test was like what I hear an "acid trip" is like, and in traffic with a lobotomy of the superego.

By the end of the first year, it was clear that Moishe's scheme — whatever it was — was panning out, and by extrapolation, by the end of 24 months, I would be the millionaire he had predicted. It was therefore time to put some serious thought into outwitting the old bastard and his stupid contract.

In the guise of doing me a favor, he had been sending me monthly statements of my incoming profits. Where he got the numbers from I don't know since all sales were between the customer and me only, with records only I kept, and assumed that only I had. Yet his figures were dead on. I figured he had a friend at the bank. I switched banks, but the accurate figures kept coming. So I had the girls help me research the question of "Swiss banking", and decided that was the way to go to maximize my privacy. Professional, discreet, secure.

Under pressure from France and especially Hitler Germany to reveal their customers, the Swiss passed the 1934 Banking Law, which made it a federal crime, punishable by imprisonment, for any banker to divulge client information, even to the Swiss government. Good thing too, since the Nazis had made foreign deposits a capital crime. And while in extreme cases of criminal activity, the Banking Law could be challenged, such exceptions were very few. Secrecy was the norm.

Further secrecy was guaranteed by having a numbered account, not linked to any name. Setting up such an account required meeting face to face with a high bank officer, and lots of authentication documents, but the results of that face to face were nowhere traceably recorded. All that was left of it was a number. A numbered account required a minimum deposit of $100,000, and had a $300/year service fee, but by my second contract year, that amount was no barrier, and by the time I would have to file my 1962 taxes the following ides of April, when one has to report all foreign deposits over $10,000, my 24 months would have expired and who knew what my world would look like then? So after New Year's day, I decided to transfer all my money to a Swiss bank numbered account.

The problem was that Sherlock Looie (who loved the intrigue) advised me that I shouldn't deposit in a Swiss bank branch in the US, since bank branches have to follow the laws of the countries in which they're located — and not those of the country where the corporate bank office is. A Swiss bank branch in the United States has no greater privacy than a regular U.S. bank does. So the family and I took a little joyride up to Montreal in our new Edsel where the girls could practice their French, Deirdre could do some faux-European shopping, and I could disappear for a few hours into the offices of the Royal Bank of Canada (Suisse) for a financial *tête a tête* with a gray-haired Monsieur.

Done. Let Moish bang his head against the Canadian Alps.

But at the end of January, he again reported absolutely accurate numbers. They even reflected cash I had stashed in the girl's accounts, and under my mattress. How he figured it, God only knows. But it was clear that my only safe strategy was to keep my accumulated income below a million dollars. That $999,999.99 was an obvious target, but to play it safe, I'd limit myself to $999,000. Which was easy enough to do by substituting give-aways for sales, potentially past that, thereby limiting my exposure, and increasing my civic charm, along with Moishe's. How could he object? He didn't.

Come mid-September next, Moish came over to my office down the street from his to congratulate me on attaining my wished-for goal. He presented his statement of my year-to-date earnings, and for the first time, his numbers did not match mine. Why? He had included the RBC (Suisse) Rosh Hashanah payment of $39,960, — its application of a 4% interest on deposits which considerably upset both Looie's and my calculations. Thus, he said, his end of the contract was fulfilled, and now it was my turn to perform. I assured him that my 24 months weren't up yet, and he reminded me of the "whichever came first" clause of the contract. I objected that the extra $40k wasn't from my sales, and he countered that it was income nonetheless, and that whatever the source, I was now the millionaire he promised. When I urged that much would be deducted in taxes, he recapitulated our previous discussion of that topic.

There was really no defensible way around it: at that moment in time, I was a millionaire, and my life quest had been attained. So now what? Moishe told me he would apply his end of the contract in ten days, on Yom Kippur.

Those ten days were a holy hell of waiting and wondering. What did that madman have in store for me as reward or punishment for my having achieved my goal — a goal, after all, which was probably the most common of all goals among mid-life American males. During that time, my baldness must have grown by 30%, my wrinkles increased by a quarter, and my nose became more bulbous. Under stress, I was aging fast. Charlie Hyde, the pre-geezer.

Even my family noticed. Five days into the ten, a family meeting was called not by me or Deirdre, but by the Oooies — the first time they had ever so asserted their hegemony. We gathered out on the back porch. It was a beautiful fall evening, but Nature's implicit agenda did not signal joy to the world, rather it's flip side: the upcoming death of life.

"Whazzup?" I began when we were all seated, trying set an upbeat tone. "Dad," Cooie the elder began, "You don't look good. You look so worried. What's going on?"

I could have denied everything, hoping that the upcoming news would be good, and I could shower them with even more riches than those they were soaked in at the moment. But somewhere, the Big Lie has to stop, and here seemed as good a place as any. I told the kids the whole story of the mysterious contract, and the source of their growing family fortune. There was a great silence on the porch. Even the crickets paused. There came a great darkness over the land. It was new moon.

"What do you know about Moish, Dad? What's his background? Where did he come from before here? Why Paterson?" A reasonable set of questions from Sherlock Looie. All of which had no answers. "How come you never asked him?" she pressed.

And the answer to that question was just as mysterious as the situation itself. How come I, who pride myself on being on top of everything, figuring all the angles, how come Charlie Hyde has allowed this most important being in his life, his goddamn boss, to walk around shrouded in such a cloud of unknowing? The answer was embarrassing.

"I dunno. He's just not the kind of guy you ask these things about. He just sort of *is*. Period. Like that thing in his office, you've seen it. The yem. The 'I yem' yem. Adorable — and unfathomable."

"Well, I think we should find out more about him if we're going to figure out what the contract implies. I'll get on it."

Dooie, the youngest, the quietest, also seemed perturbed. "Did you know we all went to one of his rallies?"

"No. Which one?"

"At Rutgers."

"I didn't see you there."

"I guess we looked like all the other students," Cooie proudly said.

"We all thought he was pret-ty strange."

"You knew that already."

"I mean *very* strange. Very. Weird, even."

Like her mother, Dooie was an antenna tuned to weirdness.

"We have to investigate him. Like HUAC, except for un-American eccentricity."

I knew Looie was only half joking, and that she spoke for all the head-nodding sisters. Evidently there was an already-conceived, pre-contract-investigation plan based only on their experience at the rally.

"And just how do you propose to do that? March up and interrogate him?"

Insulted, they proceeded, Cooie as spokeswoman.

"You've mentioned several times that he has this down-stairs office he disappears to, incommunicado, for long periods of time."

"No phone extension, and a permanent DO NOT DISTURB sign," Looie added.

"We can find out a lot by getting into that office and looking around."

After years of living with the mystery, the idea of break-ing and entering Moishe's *sanctum sanctorum* seemed beyond the pale. But the Oooie's plan seemed feasible, and they had already gathered the tools required, mainly flashlights, a flash camera borrowed from a friend, notepads and new ballpoint pens. Deirdre gave no indication of her opinion other than observing that the following night would be astrologically allowable. Propitious? She couldn't say.

So, in the early morning of day seven, 3 AM to be exact, the Oooies and their father arrived at Moish's lot. Even though I was now stationed down the street I still had my key to the old office and showroom. There was a lot of glass facing a River St., a main drag, so we had to be judicious with our use of the flashlights. But once we descended to the windowless basement, we felt free to illuminate the scene as best we could.

"Creepy," Dooie opined.

Moish's office was dead ahead. His "private leboratory". Over the outer door was a sign reading CAVE, CAVE, DOMINUS VIDET. Was this his "cave"? I understood the Latin of course, everything except why. There was no handle on the door, but it stood surprisingly open enough to get a fingerhold. The room was unexpectedly large, and housed a carved desk with a gilded clock facing the door, a clock with only an hour hand, resting close to 12. Contemplating its unequivocal assertion, I had a feeling that whatever it meant, it had nothing whatsoever to do with time.

We could see ourselves creeping around in a cheval-type mirror, the full-length kind that could tilt on a frame. But the reflecting glass was not the usual oval. Rather, it consisted of the same structure as the great sign outside the lot — ten mirrors, attached to a black steel frame — all fitted in the oval of an antique cheval in a wooden frame. Whatever that configuration meant, it seemed even more formidable in miniature than it was towering over the street.

But the most striking object in the room was a reproduction so fine that it could have been the original — of Rembrandt's painting of Belshazzer's Feast, with the astonished, turbaned king staring in horror at a hand coming out of a cloud, inscribing in gold Hebrew letters the awful four words, Mene, Mene, Tekel, Upharsin, recounted in the book of Daniel. (Praised be the Jesuits again, for my education…)

From my Bible studies, I knew the story, the scene, and what these Hebrew words meant. This was a big feast, no holds barred, so Belshazzar used the good dishes, had borrowed gold and silver cups from the Temple of Solomon to praise "the gods of gold and silver, brass, iron, wood, and stone." Somebody up high must have gotten really pissed.

Belsh called his wise men to interpret the meaning, but they were stumped. The words were just normal terms for weights and measures, "a mina, a mina, a shekel and a half shekel". Enter Daniel, who warned the king of his blasphemous folly in using the temple objects and praising their "gods". His interpretation: "Numbered, weighed, and divided." God had numbered the days of Belshazzar's kingdom, which has been weighed on the scales and found wanting, a kingdom soon, in fact, to be divided up between the Medes and the Persians.

Why this painting? What did it mean for Moish's business here? The contrast with his upstairs office was spooky. Up there, well-lit by the sun, the only art object was that skewered porcelain sweet potato. It would be five days before I understood. But even then, being in that room aroused my first premonitions of death, or being confronted with some unexpiated crime.

We were all carefully studying the painting when, from behind us, we heard a friendly voice.

"Vell, you like my penting? I did it myself, from numbers."

Moish was sitting at his desk, cigar in mouth, watching us.

"Heving fun? You vill all need a little nep tomorrow, no?"

There was no excuse. We were caught red-handed. We all just stood there in silence. Would he call the police?

"Hokay, go get some sleep. Chollie, you should come in a liddle late to voik. But before you go, I vant you should tink about vun ting, and det is dis: Mister Kafka vunce told me dere are really only two sins. All de others come from dese — impatience and laziness. Adam and his vife ver kicked out from Eden because of impatience, and dey ver too lazy to get beck. But, he said, mebby dere is only vun bigtime sin — impatience. From impatience dey ver expelled, and from impatience, dey don't get beck.

"So good night, kindeleh. Get some sleep. Yom Kippur is coming." And he laughed his big Shadow laugh. We were all adequately spooked.

12. THE TIME OF RECKONING

At dinner the next day, Looie tried to calm me down. Emotions, she advised, were antagonistic to clear reasoning. We had to look at the evidence we had discovered, and the hints we had been given. Cooie, being an expert on emotion, agreed, and Dooie zeroed in on Moish's mention of Yom Kipper. Children of her type have a keen sense of what is up.

I had always thought Yom Kipper was some kind of oily fish that only Jews could love. This Yom Kipper I was to learn otherwise. To my astonishment Yom had nothing to do with tastiness, but meant, simply, "day". But Kipper was actually Kippur, and was, alas, not a member of the finny tribe, but meant "atonement". Yom Kippur, the Day of Atonement, was the holiest day of the year for Moish and his race.

However, what he had neglected to tell me (it wasn't in the contract) was that the ten days between Rosh Hashanah and Yom Kippur, the ten days I had waited to find out my fate, were called the Days of Awe. They hadn't seemed particularly awesome to me, consumed as I was with his next move, and constrained in my sales by the freebie promises I had made.

And now that the awe-jig was up, he sat me down for the most momentous of his little lectures. The Days of Awe — now he tells me — were for exorcising all my evil spirits, begging pardon from those I had wronged, so that on Yom Kippur, today, that is, I would be able to confront God, *mano à mano*, with a clean soul so He would inscribe my name in the Book of Life for the coming year, and not in the Book of Death. So Moish and I together were going to fast all day (good thing I had had a big breakfast), and together chant all the Jewish prayers for the day.

I told him I wasn't Jewish. That he knew — it was obvious. I told him I didn't know any Jewish prayers. He said it would be a repeat-after-me affair, and he would pray them in English for my benefit. God, he said, understood English, He assured me I had to atone for my sins — or else.

He said, "I know you don't tink you sin a lot. Dis is a very popular attitude around here. But do you ever face up to de Troot? I see de enswer is no. Nobody sins, everybody sleeps good at night. No one is vicked except udder people, never you. But you hev to agree dere's some pretty schlocky business going on out dere. So unless you're different from everyone else dis is also your problem. All dese prayers are about 've', and if you tink you're not a 've', den dere about *you*. Get it? You know vhat is evading?"

I nodded.

"Here," he said, handing me a piece of paper with the

prayers. "So I don't got to repeat. I know my proniuncing is not gud American. "

I present this paper as his rap sheet on me and "de voild". I leave out the Hebrew printed above each verse.

    For using the misdeeds of others to excuse our own;

    For denying our responsibility for our own misfortunes;

    For refusing to admit our share in the troubles of others;

    For passing judgment without knowing the facts;

    For remembering the price of things but forgetting their value;

    For loving our egos better than truth.

MAY ALL WE DO TODAY RETURN US TO THE WAY, FORGIVING AND LETTING GO, RELEASING US ANEW

WE DENY THAT WHICH IS ETERNAL WHEN WE DENY OUR OWN DEPTHS: FOR THE FAILURES OF TRUTH, WE ASK FOR CLEAR VISION

    For using people as steppingstones to advancement;

    For hiding from others behind an armor of mistrust;

    For treating with arrogance people weaker than ourselves;

    For giving ourselves the fleeting pleasure of inflicting lasting hurts;

    For cynicism which eats away our faith in the possibility of love.

FOR ALL THE WAYS WE VIOLATE THE SACRED WEB, TEACH US HOW TO HEAL CREATION.

There was more. And more. And more. Evading, denying, violating! What a detestable orgy of remorse! Downright Un-American. I had to admit that if I took it *cum grano salis*, I might — might — be *slightly* guilty of some, well, many, of the things on Moishe's list. But a big time offender? No. Very small potatoes.

But I *was* getting into the swing of Yom Kippur. Maybe it was low blood sugar, but by the evening, I began to see the possibilities of the "voild" incorporating this kind of thought, and kicking off some new behavior. Moishe's group acknowledgment of sin was potentially way more powerful than creeping into some confession booth and immediately being pardoned. No wonder the world hates Jews.

As night fell, he blew his nose very loudly to end the service, and served me some getting-stale bagels and some Manischewitz wine substitute for me to break my fast with joy. He ate nothing.

"So? Are you all repented?" he asked.

I assured him I was.

"You tink I believe you?"

"No," I said, hoping it was the right answer.

"You're lucky I didn't make you sving a chicken around your head. By de vey, I don't believe you."

"So did I fail my test?"

"A big D minus for you. Foist community soivis, and den a makeup exem."

"Or? Are you going to take my million away from me?"

"You don't got no million. You don't got nothing."

"Want to see my bank book?'

"You don't got no benk book. You don't got no benk."

"I have to disagree. The Royal Bank of Canada (Suisse)…"

"Dey never hoid of you. Your name dey don't got."

"Yes I know. I have a numbered account. But surely Monsieur Frothingham knows me, and will vouch for me. I spent hours with him, talking with him, showing him all my papers."

"Too bad. He's dead, and no one else knows you."

I hadn't realized this might be a problem with the Swiss bank system. Monsieur Frothingham was aging, all right, but he wasn't *that* old. How was I to know? There must be some way…

"You mean I worked for two years selling all those Edsels for nothing?"

"You tink megically appearing cars vit megically appearing money can't just disappear — like megic?"

"But really — nothing? What will my family live on? How will we pay the mortgage? Why do you want to make people suffer?"

"You really vant to know?"

"Yes, tell me. "

"Foist of all, vhat do you know from suffering? Anybody in your house is starving, anybody is spied on by de police? Anybody locked up in a madhouse, on de vay to being deported? Anybody in a concentration kemp? Vhat do you know from suffering? Vit all your blessings, vhat have you done for udders? And don't tell me your charities. Charities from my charities. You just sleep and play and fuss and den go to sleep again. Vhy you are de vay you are? You call dis a human life, yours? Instead of a million dollehs you should have got a big potch in tuchas."

"Sorry, but I yem what I yem."

"Very funny," he says.

It was more than time for an apologue.

"Look," I told him, "I'm just a regular American human being, more or less. We all live behind the Veil of Maya." I thought I'd trump him with this. Whatever you might think about the Ten Commandments, at least there are only ten, and abstaining from obscurity is not one of them.

"Things are not what they seem. I'm actually a very nice man. I don't kill flies. I taught my children to catch them in a glass, and let them out the back door. I paid a penny a fly. You can ask them. I could be bad if I wanted. Spectacular badness is very impressive. More than spectacular goodness. But I have many desires. What's wrong with that? My chief desire was to do good for my customers, show them the real way of the world so they wouldn't go out and be cheated. Capitalism made me do it. It's a big operation.

"I'm nervous, I admit. I'm critical. I'm not over-relaxed. I thought I knew what I was doing. Find before you seek. Like that. Maybe it was just low cunning, but I assure you it was high-minded."

Moish started to yawn. Not a good sign.

"OK, maybe I have a demon self. But I also have a loving self. And a silly self. The love of screwing one's fellow man is universal. But I was more sinned against than sinning. Everyone takes advantage of me — with my inadequate theory of evil — but I don't suppose anyone gives a damn about that among the angelic orders."

He yawned dramatically.

"You accuse *me* of being spiritually asleep. How many people are *not* spiritually asleep? Huh? Do you think everyone is rushing to nourish his soul?"

To judge by his expression, I didn't seem to be winning my case, whatever it was.

"OK, maybe I've spent most of my life being an asshole, but…"

"But vhat?" It was his first comment.

"But 'he who desires and acts not breeds pestilence.' Blake."

"I hoid that my lest vacation in hell."

"You were in hell??"

He pointedly ignored me.

It seemed impossible to make a Houdini escape here. Why did I ever think a million dollars could make the difference between success and failure? You have to deal with huge forces, inside and out.

I felt like I was going nuts, as if reality was being sucked out of me into Moishe's hair. As a child, I was sometimes scared the TV or refrigerator, or some other appliance would announce a coup — like Moish — and there would be nobody there to help me, and now there was a list of their rules I had to obey. That old prophecy Daniel made to Nebuchadnezzar — that's why he had that painting in his office. 'They shall drive thee from among men,…' Maybe life on earth really *isn't* feasible.

Moishe stood up. His head seemed to touch the ceiling.

"OK, Misteh Kapisteh, you tink about it for tree days, den you come back and tell me vhat you are deciding to do."

In such circumstances, it is wise to consult some higher wisdom. My parents, and my questionable father-in-law were dead. Aunt Betsy was *non compos mentis*. Ed, Bud, and Al were hardly higher. Deirdre was mum. The girls were smart, but Christ, they were just teenagers — what did they know? If there had been a sphinx anywhere in New Jersey or the New York metropolitan area, I would have gone for a consult. Who was a wisdom figure in my life? Not Father Delaney. He'd just make me sit in his orgone box and make up dirty stories.

It came to me in a flash — a sphinx, a wisdom figure, and elder — old Dr. Williams. I heard he was sick. Maybe he'd like a visitor. I called his office, but the number wasn't answering. I called his home in Rutherford, but again, there was no answer. I began to worry.

Short of a personal visit then, I thought it appropriate to

turn to his great work about our little town, *Paterson*. I took the revered book from its central place on the mantel, closed my eyes, opened it at random in the middle, and in my simplified version of Deirdre consulting her *I Ching*, poked my finger blindly onto a page. What doth the sage have to say?

It is dangerous to leave written that which is badly written.

A chance word, upon paper, may destroy the world. Watch carefully and erase, while the power is still yours, I say to myself, for all that is put down, once it escapes, may rot its way into a thousand minds, the corn become a black smut, and all libraries, of necessity, be burned to the ground as a consequence.

Oh, the good doctor. Dr. Bill, ever so wise! Yes, a life badly written, dangerous, destroying the world, my world. Did I still have the power to erase — Moishe's Sabbath-forbidden act — before rotting a thousand minds? I closed the book, wrote a note, and went off to commit suicide.

13. [DEATH] AND TRANSFIGURATION

S ocrates. Seneca. Walter Benjamin... Suicide, the only self-respecting way to go.

You may think mine was a hasty decision, but I am the dramatic type, and believe me, the majority of suicides are as hastily decided as this. Besides, I had just lost all my money, probably my family, my last two years of work, my standing in the community, my self-respect, and I wasn't about to hang around to watch my wife and daughters starve. If Sylvia Plath could stick her head in an oven after setting out breakfast for her two little children, my kids can surely fend for themselves.

Suicide...

Paterson Falls is a sensational event in the otherwise uneventful Passaic River, densely frothing on the rocks fifty feet below, foaming over ancient stone toward a peaceful basin, and moving on, a brooding landscape, creating the shape of our town. In April, the rains melt the snow and create a mad, roaring torrent, washing tree trunks along with it, over the turmoil of the falls, dirty yellow water exploding on the rocks. By atonement-autumn the scene is calmer, but a fifty foot drop to The Valley of Rocks, is still a fifty foot drop — onto rocks — and into a tumble of spray in the void, enough to do one in. There are no Rhine maidens at the bottom.

Alexander Hamilton had been much impressed by the sight of the Great Falls of the Passaic. Its massive power, he thought, might create a great center to drive the mills of a "national manufactory" producing cotton goods, wallpapers, hats and shoes, carriages, pottery, bricks, pots, pans and all the buttons needed in the United States. Hamilton the bean-counter. I noticed it could also produce death.

Out on the parapet, comforted by the plunge of the water — a model for my life — a roll relentlessly unrolling, I climbed over the railing, walked along the cliff, picked a beach plum from a bush, and dropped it gently into the roar below, fascinated, watching it fall. Falling. The Fall. In fall.

And I listened. Was it just the water roaring, or was it some deep protest from the assaulted stones, from consciousness devoid of consciousness? Novalis once imagined stones as solidified tears and thought certain mountains looked petrified from sheer horror at the thought of humanity. Considering myself, my wasted life, I suspected he might be right.

From the height of the falls I could see the low range of Paterson's hills to the north, and over my shoulder, the little town itself, that collection of oddballs, a true paradise for fantastical characters. No wonder Moish had made such a hit. He was simply the apotheosis of all Paterson's curiosities.

A lot of charming history there. Back in '35 I saw Elmer McDuffy of the Black Yankees pitch a no-hitter against the House of David at City Stadium, the first for a colored ball club. Moish would have been embarrassed — the jungle bunnies beating the hell out of the Jews. Hell, when I was born, Paterson was a key node in the international anarchist movement until the Justice Department raids destroyed the subversive Italian community. Some justice!

Thinking such fond thoughts about my little town almost turned my intention around. Suicide does not love warmth. But staring at the falls, the drop, I felt the Imp of the Perverse tickling my inner ear and cerebellum, making me understand the inevitability of falling. I grabbed the railing above to steady myself, and held there, hyperventilating, I thought of all those other people walking around Paterson in the alarming disarray which human beings can suffer. It would be so easy, so right, to just let go and fall.

I lay there supine on the down-slanting rock face of the cliff, my arms outstretched, spread-eagled over my head, my hands still clinging to the safety rail. The Imp of the Counter-Perverse urged me to hang on, while the inverse perverse pulled at my feet, trying to dislodge them from under me. Stretched, clinging, to a Procrustean bedframe of schist. Gravity would do the rest.

Is suicide the one truly serious philosophical problem? Damn straight.

There I lay on October 10, 1962, splayed between life and death above the Paterson Falls, a car salesman divided within himself against himself like the cross I formed. *Crucifixus, etiam pro nobis.* All those painful masses swarmed through my head. Bach, Mozart, now I get it, I get it.

The cross. The cross! — why didn't I think of it? I would outstrip Jesus Who Was Called Christ! Do Him one better.: resurrection without the bother and stink of death. Here at the Falls, the cross my salvation! Just like Father Mulvaney always said, my salvation...

And if mine, the world's.

Free at last!

14. BECOMING CHRIST(LIKE)

Down with the Grand Old Duke of York and his doctrine of Halfway Up/Halfway Down! Henceforth, *nothing* by halves. Imagine if King Solomon had gone ahead and cut up the baby; some things simply can't be split down the middle. Nothing, I say, by halves.

The wages of sin is death, right?, and truly I say unto you, "Unless a grain of wheat falls into the earth and dies, it remains alone; but if it dies, it bears much fruit." John, something, something, right? Right. I would begin my *via dolorosa.*

Why hadn't I done this two years ago? Vengeance on the old me! Strike! Kill! A pack of righteous wild beasts seethed inside.

My face, I'm sure, looked equally wild, repulsive — reflecting all crimes, all deformities as I wallowed in vileness — immediate, concrete, filling my gut and surging through my veins.

Oh, Lord, destroy my vanity and any old pretensions concerning some rich and famous Charles M. Hyde. Let me disintegrate and suffer, like so many others, perhaps not on anything as illustrious as a cross, but something more down in the mire, more awash in the Void. Allow me a second birth, oh midwife Death.

OK, Charlie, calm down, enough hysteria. The real question is, In these here pricey shoes, what would Jesus do?

I would find out.

I must admit Jesus' life didn't go well. He didn't reach his earning potential. His brand was good, but he wasn't respected by his colleagues. Even his friends weren't loyal, at least when the chips were down. His life wasn't all that long, and he didn't meet his soul mate, even if he might have gotten tired of her eventually. And he wasn't even nice to his mother. So maybe he's not the best person to model.

He did say a lot of great things, though. The one I like best was "Her sins are forgiven because she loved much." I wish I had said something like that.

It just shows you have to have sinned to be forgiven. Maybe I could refashion myself as some kind of Blakean artist in Christ, binding with briars, my joys & desires. Gods are pretty strange, though. Look at Job, with his house falling on his poor daughters.

And what about my daughters? If Tolstoy can walk away from his family and still be some kind of a saint, so can I.

They'll do all right — beautiful, smart, all with that light silky skin they got from Deirdre. No problem developing Vitamin D from the sun. They'll have good pregnancies with all that D. I'll have grandchildren with good bones.

I begin to understand what Tolstoy was getting at when he called on people to stop playing at history, and begin simply to live.

So that I will do — in the footsteps of Christ — Moish the Father, I the Son, and the spirit of Dr. Will as the Holy Ghost. Being atheists, many of you may think this is ridiculous. But I refer you to the opinion of your beloved atheist, H.L. Mencken, who, when asked if he believed in baptism, replied "Believe in it? I've seen it done!"

Human misery demands a divine response – and I can be its delivery service. A *via Christi?* I shall do it! You better believe it.

14. IMITATIO CHRISTI: THE EARLY AND MIDDLE CHURCH OF HYDE

The three synoptic Gospels, and St. Paul himself, all encourage imitating Jesus in a Christian life. So the first question is, what would Jesus *wear* as a grown man or even as a child? (We would have both in our congregations, and a unisex approach to our women.)

In creating a new life, a change of dress is important. Moish said so. I remember when I was wearing knickers, how big a deal it was to get my first pair of long pants. So a foundational question for us at the beginning was "What's the one thing Jesus would have worn — lifelong?" A yarmulke, that's what — one of those little Jewish skullcaps. Skullcap. Even that *name* was a *memento mori*. This Hyde-ism thing was deep from the get-go.

The Church of Hyde began as a tiny home industry, entirely consistent with Hamilton's agenda for Paterson: a religious goods manufactory.

In such matters I knew it was critical to be ecumenical, to service all Judeo-Christians, honoring the entire heritage of

Western Civilization (Indians, excepted, of course), and thus creating the largest potential customer base. Plus including Jews in your pitch is always good business.

Church of Hyde sales began with a simple variation on the classic yarmulke, updated for an aerodynamic age. How would Edsel have imagined it? What would Edsel have worn? With our very first offering, we began what has become an international rage, and a corporation now situated — by dint of its sales, profits, assets, and market value — securely among the Forbes 500.

Stay with me here. It's easy enough to reject such a path (successful as it may have been) as crass, but we're talking about spreading Christian — nay, Judeo-Christian — morality to a resistant and sin-infested world. Would it be better just to murmur darkly among ourselves in some crumbling storefront while nations devour one another? Jesus's vision has had almost two millenia to get out there, and has it? Something new was needed. And the new is, as ever, the old: the Invisible Hand of the Marketplace.

The point is simply this — to get this stuff out there, by hook or by crook, and in this case, hopefully more hook than crook (which, after all, has poor associations.) Working as a family, right from our basement at 239 Spring St., Paterson, all five of us brainstormed, created and illustrated the first Church of Hyde Catalogue, and hand-sewed and built the first prototypes.

Fear of the obvious has been the premature death of

many a brilliant idea. We were not afraid. Who would have thought that simply adding a (Wittgenstein) propeller to an orthodox Jewish skullcap would lift it (Hegel's *aufheben*) so far out to its limiting, often alienating, divisive category to make it a universal symbol of freedom and joy? It turned out to be great for attracting the young, and assuring a massive future for the denomination.

These days, with sin abounding, a Hyde-ist[1] needs to be able to keep a cool head. Forty-five per cent of the body's heat is radiated through the scalp[2]. Disperse that heat with Star of David, Crucifixion or Hammer 'n Sickle vents and six-, three- or one-bladed propellers designed by Ludwig Wittgenstein[3]. Convection-driven. Choice of traditional black, or alternating black and white for easier decision-making. $15.95

[1] The hyphen serves to distinguish us from Deists – which we are certainly not.
[2] U.S. Army Survival Manual, 1943.
[3] Private communication from Carolyn (Cooie) Hyde)

The catalogue page illustration represented only the Old Testament version, since the others are easy to imagine. How surprised we were when the drawing created an unexpected demand for false beards and sidelocks for men and boys of any religious persuasion. Bearded children particularly love parading around. You see them everywhere now across the country and across the world. It all started here in Paterson.

Sales progress was phenomenal. From three months post-contract to its purchase two years later by Interstellar Propeller, growth was spectacular, peaking, of course, during the Christmas season, but strongly plateauing away beyond it.

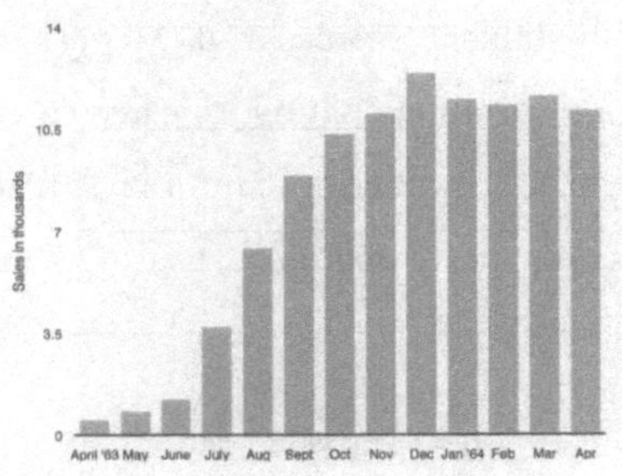

It was on this rock that we founded, (incorporated), and built my Church.

I say "my church" because the girls early on became suspicious, alas, and alienated, each in her way, and together they drifted away like a cloud on a windy day. Neither did Deirdre take all this at the right level. But as Jesus said, "If any man come to me, and hate not his father, and mother, and wife, and children, and brethren, and sisters, yea, and his own life also, he cannot be my disciple." (Luke 14:26) Family values would clearly have to be reconsidered.

On the other hand, by the time of the Interstellar Propeller takeover, I had quite a bit of money to play with, far more than that imaginary million which precipitated my change of life. My first project for the New Great Awakening was a line of religious books for gifted children, modeled on devotional books popular in the Middle Ages, combinations of breviary and primer, small modern manuscripts for lay children, and parents concerned with their spiritual welfare. I decided to publish in English, not Latin, feeling language instruction to be beyond my initial mission.

Each title featured one parable (written by myself), profusely illustrated with copyright-free artwork. Accompanying the parables were separate discussion guides in attached envelopes (created by me) for parents, but for obvious Fourth Commandment reasons, not available to the child. At one dollar each, who could refuse? Sales to parochial schools and religious home schoolers were brisk. Many of those bearded children must have pored over these texts, and experienced long bedtime sessions on the discussion points. Since I was both publisher and sole author, those dollar bills piled up, and while trivial compared to other catalogue sales, showed that the Church of Hyde was more than a retail operation, and could plunge headlong into exegesis and theology.

An illustration will show the reader the kind of thought-world we were evoking.

THE PARABLE OF THE HEDGEHOG AND THE FOX

A certain hedgehog was walking in a field when he met a fox who said, "Friend, why walkest thou so early in the morning?" The hedgehog spake, "Canst thou do anything better with your legs?" to which the arrogant fox replied, "I imagine so. My legs are so much longer than thine."

The hedgehog took affront, and he said unto the fox, "Nay…if we two were to race, I wager I would win." "Fat chance," replied the fox, "but what willst thou wager?" "If you win, I will give up unto thee one of my children for dinner," he said. "And what would you want from me, should you win?" asked the fox. "Your life."

The fox thought the terms were strange, idiosyncratic, but so sure was he of winning, he accepted the wager.

"Tomorrow morning, then, here at six," sayeth the hedgehog. "I have to rest up today to prepare for tomorrow." Much amused, the fox agreed.

Once at home, the hedgehog conspired with his wife as to how such a race might be won, and their ever-threatening enemy dispatched.

And it came to pass that the next morning, at five, the hedgehog and his wife surveyed the field on which the race was to be run, and the hedgehog spake thus unto his wife: "The fox will run in that furrow, and I in this one. Thou willst stand at the end across the field, and when the fox approaches, thou willst call out to him 'I'm here already.'"

Said fox arrived at six. The hedgehog's wife (who much resembled the hedgehog) waited in her furrow, far across the field. The race began, and the fox tore down the furrow like unto a windstorm, whilst the hedgehog ran only three steps, and returned to his place.

As the fox approached the finish line, the hedgehog's wife called out unto him, "I'm here already." The fox was breathing hard, and had no time to think or question. "All right, then, let us run back to the starting line to see who really wins." And he spun around and took off, leaving the hedgehog's wife in the dust behind him.

When the fox neared the new finish line, he saw the hedgehog ahead of him, waving and calling out "I'm here already."

The fox could not believe it. He called for a rematch, the best two out of three. "As many as you want," the hedgehog allowed.

But so hard did he run, that halfway through the homestretch of the second race, the fox's heart burst, and behold, he fell headlong into the dust. He was buried by the hedgehog and his wife and his three children from the dirtpiles which lay along the furrow, and afterward the family all returned home and rejoiced.

COMMENTARY ON THE PARABLE

First, you will notice that the vocabulary limits far exceed those of standard children's publishing, which I imagine to be a capitalist plot to dumb down the upcoming generations, the better to sell them their products. Vocabulary is the thing with which to help a child take wing. You will notice, too, the use of older second person conjugations which not only give the tale a biblical tone, but which also alert the child to the history of the language he is engaged in mastering.

But to the parable itself.

There are many variations on this story in classical fable and various vernaculars. In general, the hero of the story is seen as the humble hedgehog, who uses his brains and a clever scheme to outwit the wily and arrogant fox, and rid himself and his family of a constant, unpredictable threat. The family is now secure, the humble are exalted, and the self-exalted laid low — as Jesus would have it.

Yet we ask the modern child to consider another interpretation. Where does one draw the line between security and crime? "Thou shalt not lie" is not featured in the ten commandments, yet lying (viz. Kant) cannot be the basis for universal action. How then is one to judge the hedgehog, whose lies eventuate in a capital (if plausibly deniable) crime?

We at the Church of Hyde, believe every child should struggle with such moral dilemmas, and we hold no brief for either side. In America, each is entitled to his own opinion, and Romans 5:12 notwithstanding, we are all innocent until proven guilty. A delinquent child addicted to trespass may grow into a Luther or a Nietzsche. The created world could use more such transgressors.

AUFHEBUNG

Things began to truly *aufhebe* with the establishment of WWJD, 940 AM, Paterson. As you are not likely to know, not having been educated by Jesuits, "*Aufhebung*" is Hegel's famous term for the engine which drives the synthesis of opposites, the raising of things to higher levels, taking them a step further, in the dialectical dance. (I always loved engines.) For "*Aufhebung*", you sometimes hear the word "sublation" if you inhabit sublationary circles, but who does? Americans should damn well learn the Kraut word, which is better than anything we've got. What word do we have which combines negating, preserving, and refashioning all in one? For Hegel, as for Whitman, self-contradiction is not only legitimate, but necessary for growth and progress, for living in freedom in a rational community. Power, as my daughter Looie might say, to the Aufhebes!

Negating, preserving and refashioning all went into the miraculous growth of Hydianity. Using an initial splash of provocative "things" to build a bank account, and upping the dimensions to literary/philosophical interpretations for added respectability, the next step, going on, but preserving while refashioning, was to really get the good news out there — evangelism, (Church latin, from the Greek *evangelion* good news, from *eu-* + *angelos* messenger), spreading of the word and making it well-muscled flesh as quickly as possible.

This required a mass media consultant, and who was more the expert on catchy, effective, overwhelmingly impressive ads, but Moish? So I returned to the kingdom of my tormentor — and it was…gone! Both the larger once-Edsel lot, and its smaller progenitor, up the street — gone. What the hell! I had driven and walked past them many times during my exile. I had seen the flags flying and the statue flashing one light or another even the week before, and noted how, after my leadership, the once-Edsel lot seemed to have collapsed back into a pre-visionary century in which Moish perhaps, but not the cars themselves, ruled. But now even the statue was gone, stolen away. Instead, signs indicating that the lots were to let, and all debt to the previous owners was deemed forgiven. There wasn't much debt, since we usually had dealt in cash, and the little there was was owed to Moish personally, so I guess he could forgive it. But still, where was he? Where was my expert consultant? Disappeared into some cloud from whence he came?

So there I was, graduated, on my own two feet yet again, cast off into the wilderness of 1960s secular America, needing to hang my theses on the doors of quick food restaurants and cathode ray screens.

But — another wise decision — I would start with radio, a medium I understood from deep in my childhood days, my teachers pre-Moish, better-than-Moish: Amos, Andy, Sam Spade, Baby Snooks, The Creaking Door, Fibber McGee, The Shadow, Mr. Keen, Jack Benny, Inner Sanctum, Henry Morgan, The FBI in Peace and War.

But topping them all: I was twenty years old when Orson Welles scared the shit out of the whole country, but especially the citizens of New Jersey, locus of his alien invasion. What inspiration, what a lesson on how art can function to create panic. TV would be a different story later on, and a poor second.

So — WWJD, 940 on your AM dial, Paterson, New Jersey. I saw it first as a money-raising extender. Our audience had inherited the prosperous 50s. But unfortunately those with money to spare had also inherited the rationing war years, and some even the great depression, still saving string and peeling the tin foil off gum sticks and cigarette wrappings. But as an income source for the new world a-coming, they had to be hauled on board.

It wasn't that hard, since religion holds all the face cards. It just has to announce the good news. I bought five minutes twice a day, seven days a week. Because in the world of religious belief, self-deception is a very real and well-known possibility, the program was titled "In Search of Truth", spoken by a deep God-voice over a full Hammond organ rendition of Bach's great chorale, *Jesu, Meine Freude,* music in and under, announcer, music back up to full, the magic of Bach guaranteeing optimum attention.

Note the brilliance here (even if I have to say so myself). Without any hints from Moish, and avoiding much of his crassness, the Bach introduced several levels of subliminal persuasion. First the choice of music itself, its clarity, certainty, and total affirmation. Second, the fact that the audience by and large didn't know what the music was, and so underestimated the caliber of the weapon trained on them. Finally, the finale to the introduction: "This program is offered in our common search for the Guiding Light" delivered in the same authoritative voice, pre-empting any suspicion of lesser motives.

Well, not "finally". "Finally" was the standard closing line, "Do you really want to get where you are going?" this time followed by the last three phrases of the Bach chorale, bringing to a symmetric conclusion the ABA structure of the day. There's nothing like form to bolster content. Not bad, eh?

The content itself was consistent, yet varied. It began with a simple context for requesting money to build the Church. Jesus was a great talker, producing wonderful copy I could use free of charge:

If people — especially poorer people — were worried about sending money, "Blessed are the poor" was both flattering, and a ward against post-contribution remorse. For those who needed a little more suasion, "Do not lay up for yourselves treasures on earth, where moth and rust consume and where thieves break in and steal." Rather, "consider the lilies of the field, how they grow; they neither toil nor spin; yet I tell you, even Solomon in all his glory was not arrayed like one of these," usually did the trick. At least contributions rose considerably after this thought was introduced.

Weekend contributions were usually smaller than those on weekdays. I wondered if sabbath practices might be the cause. So for a short time I usually mentioned that Jesus was notorious for ignoring the Sabbath rest, as social taboos as such meant nothing to him. *The Sabbath was made for man, not man for the Sabbath.* We stopped after we got calls from a dozen priests and ministers, and from Paterson's only rabbi.

Good old Jesus: always hanging around with the poor. Never with the rich. His various stump speeches all had terrific lines which generated my four-minute homilies:

"Man shall not live by bread alone, but by every word that proceeds from the mouth of God."

or

"I tell you, it is easier for a camel to go through the eye of a needle than for a rich man to enter the kingdom of heaven." (People seem to love that camel!)

or

"Do not be anxious about tomorrow, for tomorrow will be anxious for itself. Let the day's own trouble be sufficient for the day."

or

"Every valley shall be exalted, and the mountains and hills laid low." For those who thought this might be about end-of-time earthquakes, we explicated the text for its class-struggle import.

After a while, though, contributions began to drop off. Perhaps people had given all they had. You can't, after all, continue to wring blood from stones. But Looie, at least, the only one of the girls still paying some attention, thought blood from stones an interesting question to be solved. She evoked the common dialectic of "give and take". Not quite an *Aufhebung*, but she noticed I was proposing all give and no take for them, and that the equation had to be more balanced.

Thus was born, with more than a nod to John Calvin and the Buddha, the Church of Hyde's karma gospel of "what goes around comes around," with its essential corollary of "become spiritually richer by becoming materially poorer."

I invited my listeners to "sow some money as seed, and experience what God makes happen." All was legal, and the Church of Hyde was registered as a religious institution, so all donations were tax-deductible. Our radio services invoked only truly-held belief, and nothing that was illegal. Our Lady of Compound Interest, freely and often referred to, was the modern miracle of loaves and fishes, creating huge bounty from listeners' small financial donations.

"May great things happen" was, unlike Maharishi-fraud's Transcendental Meditation (™!) mantras (which Dooie wanted me to try) a meaningful, English language phrase in the hortatory subjunctive, understandable, and desired by all. Inviting the blessings of God in return for a combination of faith, positive speech, and donations to the Church of Hyde, made good sense to many sensible people, and an increase in material wealth was a natural hope for those who practiced such actions. *"Unless a grain of wheat falls into the earth and dies, it remains alone; but if it dies, it bears much fruit."* I already said that, but it bears saying again. "So send your grains and seeds in any denomination to the denomination of most fertile ground — the Church of Hyde."

And behold! When listeners were given the chance to become much richer by becoming slightly poorer, they went for it like the Gadarene Swine (Mark 5) plunging into the sea. I would give my poorer listeners an opportunity to attain the kind of indifference to worldly goods which might qualify them to receive Jesus message. But first, they had to be freed by me from the temptations of avarice and luxury, seduced away from whatever worldly desires and frivolous pastimes they had, so that they might recognize their abject condition and sense their need for a new, God-sent leader.

It worked, damn it, it worked! Our revenues shot up. I invested in my own TV broadcasting station, WWJD-TV, Channel 11, Paterson NJ. And thus I learned the lesson of "Be careful what you wish for."

My earliest experiences with the new broadcast medium were in the late forties, peering at snowy 10" screens, and dismissing them as a fad soon to be forgotten. Needless to say, I was wrong. By the early fifties, screen size had grown along with camera technology, and truly visionary geniuses of Orson Welles magnitude began to appear. Ernie Kovacs, Sid Caesar — it didn't get better than that. In fact, it got much worse. Videotape was developed in '57, and grew ever more useful on the production end. By the time of WWJD-TV, the snappy slickness of filmed and edited TV productions made our shows look funky. True, some of our viewers enjoyed the "nostalgic" aspect, but those were the graying toughies who wouldn't give up their record players for "stereos", or their 78s for 33s.

A new medium. I wasn't as telegenic as Meshugeneh Moish, and the message of Jesus was never as flashy as the chrome on the late-model cars. But that wasn't what started the trouble.

What started the trouble was the urgency — the same urgency I brought to my teaching — to reach out and touch people to heal them. Heal them of ignorance, yes, of course, as ever, but beyond that, of their mental and physical afflictions.

I never personally felt like a "healer" in the Deirdre or even Dooie sense. If I had, I would have gone to Rutgers medical school. But I did truly feel the healing spirit of Jesus working through me — at least at a grade B level. What I mean is, my *hubris* was moderate at most: I never tried exorcising evil spirits or raising the dead over TV. I simply invited any of the truly faithful, anyone full of guilt or self-loathing or with a less-than-lethal disease, to touch my proffered hand (tight closeup) and absorb the healing energy of Jesus right through the phosphorescent screen. I figured — on some New Jersey level of judgment — that all those high-energy electrons coming at them would surely be capable of something. I would ask "Can you feel the Jesus energy flowing through the glass?" Many of my viewers called to assure me they could. And when they followed up those calls asking whether they should see their doctors, I would tell them that the sickness, pain, and sin they were suffering from had no objective reality and that Christ came to provide spiritual and physical healing by correcting their wrong perceptions. And when they asked "So should I see my doctor or not? I don't really have the money," my pity overflowed. "First give Jesus a chance. Send only a dollar or two here as a pledge of your faith, and see what happens when you are washed in the blood of the lamb." Was this some kind of crime? *Homo sum, humani nihil a me alienum puto.* People have given money to men more crooked than Charles Hyde. But that's when the white coats jumped. "Practicing medicine without a license!"

I, personally me, little ol' Rev. Charlie Hyde, became the object of a two-year long politico-philosophico-ad hominum attack for my offering to try — note!: to *try* — to help the poor who could not afford the exorbitant fees of official medical practitioners. I, who believed not only in the efficacy of Jesus the Christ, but in the possible powers of electromagnetic radiation. I, who tendered care along with information services, and whose half-hour TV programs lasted far longer than the average office call. Office call? I, who in the day when doctors seem too lazy to leave their offices, or too cheap to spend gas money driving around to see the poor, or those too sick to get out of bed, I, I, was happy to come right into all their homes, three times a week, free of charge, to spend time with them when their own doctors required a month lead time to get an appointment, so urgent were their golf club dates.

This was simply a shameless attack on a threat of competition, motivated only by money, not by concern for the patient. If the doctors were so concerned, why didn't they ever stop by, free of charge, the way old Doc Bill did, to see how their patients were doing? Their attack on me was a vicious melange of half-truths, insulting language, and anti-religious secularist prejudice. Practicing medicine without a license? Did I ever use drugs, or leeches, or cut people up to see what would happen? Yet I was attacked as a potential killer — as if I were some rabid dog. This, from an organization which accepted advertising from tobacco companies, and whose members appeared on network television in white coats espousing the health benefits of radiation! It was all beneath contempt, and doesn't even deserve a response. Was there no room for Jesus on the Aesculapian throne? What arrogance! What restraint of trade!

Nevertheless, here I am in jail. Wilhelm Reich died in the Lewisburg Federal Penitentiary a few years ago, and they are hoping the same for me here at Northern State Prison in Newark. Will I get community service credit for my ministering to my fellow victims? Probably not.

15. SALVATOR MUNDI

In Europe, centuries ago in the era before our corrupt legal system took hold, a person's guilt or innocence was established by "ordeal." For example, someone accused of murder or sorcery was lowered into water which had been blessed. And dunking was not the only means of discovering justice. Many local rules prevailed. A free man, not subject to a feudal lord, usually had to pull a stone out of boiling water or else grab red-hot metal from a fire and carry the glowing metal at least nine paces. This kind of a system rendered all verdicts Godly and therefore final. When, for instance, Charlemagne divided up his kingdom, he specified that 'if there is any dispute over boundaries that the testimony of men cannot resolve, then the question shall be put to the judgment of the Cross'. Rival claimants had to stand in church during Mass, arms stretched out like crucified men. The man who lasted longest won. Case closed.

What was my test? I was never even invited to sit for an exam, I was simply pounced on like perhaps the criminal I once was. But even once-upon-a-time shit rises to the top, and like a prodigal son, and I will rise again and prevail.

Little do they know that this so-called scandal, completely manufactured, was designed precisely to produce the current result: Here I sit now, a Christian martyr jailed for my religious beliefs, this Calvary episode exciting a media frenzy and fueling fundraising and grassroots recruitment to unheard of heights. Mine is a case of religious persecution that is striking fear in the hearts of all Americans, a chilling case of a federal judge's insane overreach in his struggle to skunk my right to religious freedom. Bigotry and intolerance think they have won. *Optimus ridet qui ultimus ridet.*

Brothers and sisters in Christ! We have to draw the line when the courts start telling us how to run our own religious institutions — trying to close them down and destroy them. There is a "higher law", far above earthly law — and secular institutions must obey it. I've been publicly humiliated, forced off the air, and most importantly forced to deny my services to the sick and needy.

For some reason the government is ok with my selling them useless tschotkies, or books over their children's heads, or asking for money in return for unspecified blessings. No competition there to be threatened.

But just try to go up against the aggressive ignorance of the doctors. Don't they teach them the meaning of "cath" in "cathode rays"? Do they think the Cathars were just some fly-by-night sect? Are their "catheters" dedicated solely to micturation? Is it only Catholics who understand these things? Wait till my lawyers hit them with my suit for religious prejudice, persecution, and mental anguish. You, up there, wherever you are in your delusional black-robed system, know that there is *no* authority except what God has established! Medicine is too important to be left to MDs!

Calm down, Charlie, calm down, and amen. Remember it is the U.S. Constitution that protects you. "Congress shall make no law respecting an establishment of religion, or prohibiting the free exercise thereof...."

I look around me at my tier mates, and what do I see? Outcasts, publicans and sinners and possibly a male harlot — just the company Jesus loved to keep.

I am reminded of a wonderful poster a viewer sent me last week, something to the effect of "Reward for information leading to the arrest and conviction of Jesus of Nazareth, accused of anarchistic tendencies, conspiring against the state, and practicing medicine without a license. Profession: carpenter. Religious belief: Jewish. Scars on hands and feet. Aliases: Son of Man, Messiah, Prince of Peace. No fixed address. Warning: dangerous agitator. The public is asked to report any relevant information to their nearest police station."

You can learn a lot about Jesus in prison. He would be here, too. A true Christian rejoices when he hears the cell doors slam, and keys turned in the locks. *'Blessed are you when men revile you and persecute you and utter all kinds of evil against you falsely on my account.*" He told us that. And I tell myself the same thing here in our Empire of Darkness.

Last March, Dr. Bill died. Another light goes out in the world. And yesterday, Kennedy assassinated, another anti-Catholic move. At least it wasn't Moish.

I will make all this clear. But it would be good to collect my soul before my mouth reveals and my finger points to what is hidden.

APOLOGIA PRO VITA MEA

Apologia doesn't mean to apologize, for what have I to apologize for? The word comes from the Greek *apologos* "an account or story". *Apologia* does not require me to express remorse for anything.

Look, I don't want to hide behind religious tchotchkes, or new parables for smart kids, or Moishish advertising, or German idealism. I've got my own idealism, and here it is:

Jesus was reckoned to be a transgressor — and so am I. His behavior was judged criminal — and so is mine. But behavior deemed criminal by one society may be considered praiseworthy in another. And so will mine, I swear to God. Luther was able to see his own image in that of the crucified Christ, and so can I.

Like Him, I seek total renewal of the human heart, and that inevitably will mean destruction of the old ways and judgments. But unlike Him, perhaps, I don't want to become an object of veneration. I'm not asking to be deified. My mother was no virgin, and I do resemble my father. Were I to be deified, it would absolve my community from the severe demands of following in my footsteps — for how then are a collection of scatterbrained morons to measure up? And when imitation becomes impossible, my achievements will likely be transubstantiated into plain old storefront grace to be ladled out by stick-shaking priests. Oh, what a fall will be there, my countrymen! All those holy deeds, great and small, turned into paintings and statues and tchotchkes, always tchotchkes, ever more tchotchkes! Not for me. Not for the modern tragic hero, in the footsteps of Christ.

And I won't be so perfect as to demand the impossible from my followers. No wonder Jesus was crucified! Love thy enemy? Turn the other cheek? Return good for evil? Tell it to the Marines! And no more priests! Only us rabbis, teachers — like Moish. A great tradition since the fall of the temple.

Gimme that ol' time religion,
Gimme that ol' time religion,
Gimme that ol' time religion,
it's good enough for me.

Yowsah!

Guards! Guards! I snap my fingers at your red tape. Father forgive them, for they know not. Nietzsche said the last Christian died on the cross. Well, that is true no longer. As Dr. Bill once said, "What power has love but forgiveness?"

Out of the depths I will organize a megachurch, based on this book I have scribbled here in Newark's celebrated Northern State Prison.

My family, behold your father. Moish, Deirdre, Cooie, Looie and Dooie having forsaken me in my hour of need, I must needs be my own Matthew, Mark, Luke, and John. You, my readers, and all you ex-listeners and viewers out there will be my parishioners. The Church of Hyde will be born again, and if you buy this book, tomorrow you will be with me in Paradise. Into your book-holding hands, I commend my spirit — until I get out.

Bedlamite Moish wherever you are — though you, like John Milton, may be of the Devil's Party — even into *your* hands I commend my spirit.

When you think about it, Reality stinks. You know, the audible-visible-edible-intelligible world. SEMPER IN EXCRETIA SUMUS SOLIM PROFUNDUM VARIAT. Want to know what that sign over my desk meant, illiterati? We are always buried in shit. Only the depth varies. Does that affront you, o Mankind? Too bad. I am supremely indifferent to your profligate opinions. Everything sounds better in living Latin, see? But now I can confess: I told my curious customers it meant We are always under the profound rays of the sun. Which is also true, so *te absolvo*, Charlie. Go in peace.

My new dream is clearly better. Maybe all dreams are better, but mine is surely better than most. My soul doth magnify the Lord. It's nice being the only sound nut in a hatful of cracked ones.

My fangèd critics in the world of actuality, those fugitives from the law of averages? I brush them aside. They do not reach me any more than little Dooie's hand reaching for the moon. That's just life. Is it fair? No. But I don't let it drive me nuts. Though I may be an object of great suspicion, I am not a crook in any deep sense. I am not an evil person.

Jail? Scandal? Well, as they say, all publicity is good publicity, and no news is ever good news. So let it be, let it be. All will be well. Let them all load up on Miltown, for Christ's sake! Don't blame the mirror if your face is crooked.

The Lord, you see, hath shown his strength — and now He will scatter the proud — that's you! — in the imagination of their hearts.

I know my constant association with customer shortsightedness, manipulativeness and petty greed has sharpened my mind until everything presents itself in a most unsentimental light. Out there in "freedom" I felt like I was breathing collective denial and used-up air. The world has been getting on with going crazy since caves were invented, and it is already 200 years since the Grecian Urn has been cracked. As Kant says, *Aus so krummen Holze, als woraus der Mensch gemacht ist, kann nichts ganz Gerades gezimmert werden.* That's you, brothers and sisters, crooked timber out of which no straight thing can be made. So proud you are of being stupid, making huge efforts to misunderstand, with those hideous sneers on your faces, as friendly as Iago.

The Lord hath put down the mighty from their seat, and hath exalted the humble and meek. So if I am not to be God's messenger, who is left but the devil?

I stare out at the clock on the cellblock wall. The movement of that minute hand feels threatening — like a sword of Justice. When I watch it, I do expect it to jerk ahead, and slice off another minute from the future. But when it does, it stops with such an sinister quiver that my heart shudders along with it. I should stop watching it. That clock.

For reasons not entirely clear to me, He hath filled the hungry with good things and the rich He hath sent empty away. *My* reasons, however, are lucid — if someone is not at the table, he is usually on the menu. Not for JC, this. Render unto Caesar...

Of the few historical figures comparable with Jesus, only Socrates suffered a similar end, accused of godlessness and of corrupting youth, and condemned to death. The old faggot voluntarily drank the hemlock. I shall not.

But all prisoners are Jesus, and I too am a tragic hero in this passion drama. The Lord is strange. He punishes us for what is good in us as well as for what is evil and perverse. And so I am punished for my goodness. Any vileness, I commend to my conscience. It is accomplished.

Glory be to the father
And to the Son

And to the Holy Ghost.
As it was in the beginning
Is now, and ever shall be.
Amen.
Free at last!

(Behind this, I hear Moishe's laughter.)

MANY THANKS

to the Wednesday Morning Book Club at Pierson Library
(Anne August, Mickey Allgaier, Connie Bonaccio, Carol
Casey, Carol Kogut, Linda Watts),

and the Fletcher Free Library Book Discussion Group
(Nancy Ellis, Ellen Sklar, Janet Whatley, Bart Whearty) for
their criticism and corrections to the manuscript of HYDE,

to Pete Garritano for a 101 on used car salesmanship,

to Tom Hyde for a close reading, and not taking offense
at the use of his name,

and to Mark Hage for his close-editing, late-night eye.

Fomite

About Fomite

A fomite is a medium capable of transmitting infectious organisms from one individual to another.

"The activity of art is based on the capacity of people to be infected by the feelings of others." Tolstoy, *What Is Art?*

Writing a review on Amazon, Good Reads, Shelfari, Library Thing or other social media sites for readers will help the progress of independent publishing. To submit a review, go to the book page on any of the sites and follow the links for reviews. Books from independent presses rely on reader to reader communications.

For more information or to order any of our books, visit
http://www.fomitepress.com/our_books.html

More Titles from Fomite...

Novels

Joshua Amses — *During This, Our Nadir*
Joshua Amses — *Ghatsr*
Joshua Amses — *Raven or Crow*
Joshua Amses — *The Moment Before an Injury*
Jaysinh Birjepatel — *Nothing Beside Remains*
Jaysinh Birjepatel — *The Good Muslim of Jackson Heights*
David Brizer — *Victor Rand*
Paula Closson Buck — *Summer on the Cold War Planet*
Dan Chodorkoff — *Loisaida*
David Adams Cleveland — *Time's Betrayal*
Jaimee Wriston Colbert — *Vanishing Acts*
Roger Coleman — *Skywreck Afternoons*
Marc Estrin — *Hyde*
Marc Estrin — *Kafka's Roach*
Marc Estrin — *Speckled Vanities*
Zdravka Evtimova — *In the Town of Joy and Peace*
Zdravka Evtimova — *Sinfonia Bulgarica*
Daniel Forbes — *Derail This Train Wreck*
Greg Guma — *Dons of Time*

Fomite

Richard Hawley — *The Three Lives of Jonathan Force*
Lamar Herrin — *Father Figure*
Michael Horner — *Damage Control*
Ron Jacobs — *All the Sinners Saints*
Ron Jacobs — *Short Order Frame Up*
Ron Jacobs — *The Co-conspirator's Tale*
Scott Archer Jones — *And Throw Away the Skins*
Scott Archer Jones — *A Rising Tide of People Swept Away*
Julie E. Justicz — *Degrees of Difficulty*
Maggie Kast — *A Free Unsullied Land*
Darrell Kastin — *Shadowboxing with Bukowski*
Coleen Kearon — *#triggerwarning*
Coleen Kearon — *Feminist on Fire*
Jan English Leary — *Thicker Than Blood*
Diane Lefer — *Confessions of a Carnivore*
Rob Lenihan — *Born Speaking Lies*
Douglas Milliken — *Our Shadow's Voice*
Colin Mitchell — *Roadman*
Ilan Mochari — *Zinsky the Obscure*
Peter Nash — *Parsimony*
Peter Nash — *The Perfection of Things*
George Ovitt — *Stillpoint*
George Ovitt — *Tribunal*
Gregory Papadoyiannis — *The Baby Jazz*
Pelham — *The Walking Poor*
Andy Potok — *My Father's Keeper*
Frederick Ramey — *Comes A Time*
Joseph Rathgeber — *Mixedbloods*
Kathryn Roberts — *Companion Plants*
Robert Rosenberg — *Isles of the Blind*
Fred Russell — *Rafi's World*
Ron Savage — *Voyeur in Tangier*
David Schein — *The Adoption*
Lynn Sloan — *Principles of Navigation*
L.E. Smith — *The Consequence of Gesture*
L.E. Smith — *Travers' Inferno*
L.E. Smith — *Untimely RIPped*
Bob Sommer — *A Great Fullness*

Fomite

Tom Walker — *A Day in the Life*

Susan V. Weiss —*My God, What Have We Done?*

Peter M. Wheelwright — *As It Is On Earth*

Suzie Wizowaty — *The Return of Jason Green*

Poetry

Anna Blackmer — *Hexagrams*

Antonello Borra — *Alfabestiario*

Antonello Borra — *AlphaBetaBestiaro*

Antonello Borra — *The Factory of Ideas*

L. Brown — *Loopholes*

Sue D. Burton — *Little Steel*

David Cavanagh— *Cycling in Plato's Cave*

James Connolly — *Picking Up the Bodies*

Greg Delanty — *Loosestrife*

Mason Drukman — *Drawing on Life*

J. C. Ellefson — *Foreign Tales of Exemplum and Woe*

Tina Escaja/Mark Eisner — *Caida Libre/Free Fall*

Anna Faktorovich — *Improvisational Arguments*

Barry Goldensohn — *Snake in the Spine, Wolf in the Heart*

Barry Goldensohn — *The Hundred Yard Dash Man*

Barry Goldensohn — *The Listener Aspires to the Condition of Music*

R. L. Green — *When You Remember Deir Yassin*

Gail Holst-Warhaft — *Lucky Country*

Raymond Luczak — *A Babble of Objects*

Kate Magill — *Roadworthy Creature, Roadworthy Craft*

Tony Magistrale — *Entanglements*

Gary Mesick — *General Discharge*

Andreas Nolte — *Mascha: The Poems of Mascha Kaléko*

Sherry Olson — *Four-Way Stop*

Brett Ortler — *Lessons of the Dead*

Aristea Papalexandrou/Philip Ramp — *Μας προσπερνά/It's Overtaking Us*

Janice Miller Potter — *Meanwell*

Janice Miller Potter — *Thoreau's Umbrella*

Philip Ramp — *The Melancholy of a Life as the Joy of Living It Slowly Chills*

Joseph D. Reich — *A Case Study of Werewolves*

Joseph D. Reich — *Connecting the Dots to Shangrila*

Joseph D. Reich — *The Derivation of Cowboys and Indians*

Fomite

Joseph D. Reich — *The Hole That Runs Through Utopia*
Joseph D. Reich — *The Housing Market*
Kenneth Rosen and Richard Wilson — *Gomorrah*
Fred Rosenblum — *Vietnumb*
David Schein — *My Murder and Other Local News*
Harold Schweizer — *Miriam's Book*
Scott T. Starbuck — *Carbonfish Blues*
Scott T. Starbuck — *Hawk on Wire*
Scott T. Starbuck — *Industrial Oz*
Seth Steinzor — *Among the Lost*
Seth Steinzor — *To Join the Lost*
Susan Thomas — *In the Sadness Museum*
Susan Thomas — *The Empty Notebook Interrogates Itself*
Paolo Valesio/Todd Portnowitz — *La Mezzanotte di Spoleto/Midnight in Spoleto*
Sharon Webster — *Everyone Lives Here*
Tony Whedon — *The Tres Riches Heures*
Tony Whedon — *The Falkland Quartet*
Claire Zoghb — *Dispatches from Everest*

Stories

Jay Boyer — *Flight*
L. M Brown — *Treading the Uneven Road*
Michael Cocchiarale — *Here Is Ware*
Michael Cocchiarale — *Still Time*
Neil Connelly — *In the Wake of Our Vows*
Catherine Zobal Dent — *Unfinished Stories of Girls*
Zdravka Evtimova —*Carts and Other Stories*
John Michael Flynn — *Off to the Next Wherever*
Derek Furr — *Semitones*
Derek Furr — *Suite for Three Voices*
Elizabeth Genovise — *Where There Are Two or More*
Andrei Guriuanu — *Body of Work*
Zeke Jarvis — *In A Family Way*
Arya Jenkins — *Blue Songs in an Open Key*
Jan English Leary — *Skating on the Vertical*
Marjorie Maddox — *What She Was Saying*
William Marquess — *Boom-shacka-lacka*
Gary Miller — *Museum of the Americas*

Fomite

Jennifer Anne Moses — *Visiting Hours*
Martin Ott — *Interrogations*
Christopher S. Peterson — *Amoebic Simulacra*
Jack Pulaski — *Love's Labours*
Charles Rafferty — *Saturday Night at Magellan's*
Ron Savage — *What We Do For Love*
Fred Skolnik— *Americans and Other Stories*
Lynn Sloan — *This Far Is Not Far Enough*
L.E. Smith — *Views Cost Extra*
Caitlin Hamilton Summie — *To Lay To Rest Our Ghosts*
Susan Thomas — *Among Angelic Orders*
Tom Walker — *Signed Confessions*
Silas Dent Zobal — *The Inconvenience of the Wings*

Odd Birds
William Benton — *Eye Contact: Writing on Art*
Micheal Breiner — *the way none of this happened*
J. C. Ellefson — *Under the Influence: Shouting Out to Walt*
David Ross Gunn — *Cautionary Chronicles*
Andrei Guriuanu and Teknari — *The Darkest City*
Gail Holst-Warhaft — *The Fall of Athens*
Roger Lebovitz — *A Guide to the Western Slopes and the Outlying Area*
Roger Lebovitz — *Twenty-two Instructions for Near Survival*
dug Nap— *Artsy Fartsy*
Delia Bell Robinson — *A Shirtwaist Story*
Peter Schumann — *Belligerent & Not So Belligerent Slogans from the Possibilitarian Arsenal*
Peter Schumann — *Bread & Sentences*
Peter Schumann — *Charlotte Salomon*
Peter Schumann — *Faust 3*
Peter Schumann — *Planet Kasper, Volumes One and Two*
Peter Schumann — *We*

Plays
Stephen Goldberg — *Screwed and Other Plays*
Michele Markarian — *Unborn Children of America*

Essays
Robert Sommer — *Losing Francis: Essays on the Wars at Home*